Dragontide's Revenge

Dragontide's Revenge

The Third Book of Dragontide

Connie Myres

FEATHER AND FERMION PUBLISHING
MICHIGAN, USA

Feather and Fermion Publishing

Connie S. Myres
Michigan, USA
ConnieMyres.com

ISBN: 978-1-957819-27-3 (eBook)
ISBN: 978-1-957819-29-7 (hardcover)
ISBN: 978-1-957819-30-3 (paperback)

To my family and friends—
especially my sons, Lucas and Charles Kraus,
and to Lydia Kraus, Charles' wife—
thank you for your loyal support and constant
encouragement of all my projects.
I appreciate you more than words can say.

PROLOGUE

Pryce Harper-Green had heard the story countless times—how his mother, Eloise, had ventured into the forbidden Thornveil Wilds to save her dying grandfather. Armed with nothing but determination and the ancient Seafarer's Sigil she'd found glowing in an iceberg. How she'd faced forest guardians, navigated treacherous bogs, and encountered the great dragon Aurathorn himself. The Dragonscale Moss she'd retrieved had created enough Elixiron to heal Grandpa Joe.

While his mother had married his father, Tyler, after their reunion from the Dragonspine War, and while the village had celebrated their newfound prosperity, darker forces had taken notice of the young woman who carried dragon's blood in her veins.

That attention had eventually fallen on Pryce himself.

Six months ago, a storm dragon had crashed in the heart of Crystal Shores. Against all wisdom, Pryce had formed a bond with the creature he'd named

Stormwing—a connection that should have been impossible for an untrained Shorling youth. That bond had drawn the attention of Princess Seren of the Dragonkin, who'd arrived with promises of training and whispers of destiny.

What followed had been his greatest triumph and his most shameful failure. The Dragonkin had nearly transformed him into one of their own, scales spreading across his skin as he drank their corrupted potions. He'd believed their lies about protecting Crystal Shores from Seadrake Corsairs, had even agreed to marry Princess Seren—only to discover the invasion plans hidden in their war rooms. The dragon-magic ore beneath his village had been their true prize all along.

The final battle had raged across water and sky. His mother had once again risked everything to save him, following him to the Dragonkin fortress of Drakemere Island and later to Dragon's Fang Island itself. Together with young Jorr, and the mighty dragon Ragnarok, they'd exposed the Dragonkin's deception and rallied Crystal Shores' defenders. The village had survived, but at a cost—buildings burned, trust shattered, and Pryce himself forever changed by the scales that still marked his jawline.

Princess Seren had retreated with her fleet, but not before promising that their conflict was far from over. The pendant his mother had given him—filled with their family's blood mixed with draconic essence—had helped save him from complete transformation.

Now, Pryce stood on Crystal Shores' rebuilt docks and wondered if the peace they'd fought so hard to preserve was about to shatter once again.

CHAPTER 1

Pryce Harper-Green squinted at the block of greenheart he'd clamped to two sawhorses on the Island of Emberfall. One day—if the stars, the wind, and an improbable amount of spare time aligned—the rough plank would become the new figurehead for the sloop Swiftwind. The old vessel floated at anchor in Emberfall's cove, patched enough to sail but still missing the proud storm dragon prow it had lost in the last raid. At the moment the carving looked less like a fearsome drake and more like a turnip that had sprouted fangs.

"That nose still belongs on a cabbage," Kai Frostborne called from atop the paddock fence, where he pretended to supervise. A hammer dangled in his fist as he balanced on the top rail.

Pryce set his gouge, wiped a curl of wood from his brow, and spoke through a crooked grin. "Better a carved cabbage than whatever happened to your face naturally." He blew sawdust from the groove he'd been working, sending a small cloud toward his friend.

"Perfection like this is hand crafted by the gods, not by fishermen who've gone suddenly artistic," Kai said, running a hand down his jawline. "Some of us are born beautiful. Others just . . ." he gestured at Pryce's carving, "hack at wood and hope for the best."

"At least the wood stays put when I'm working on it." Pryce selected a smaller gouge for the dragon's eyes. "Unlike certain fence-sitters who can't even—"

A copper dragonet—Jorr's newest rescue, Emberstriker—chose that moment to poke its head through the fence rails. With lightning quickness, it seized the hem of Kai's tunic between needle-sharp teeth.

"Hey! You little—" Kai's arms windmilled as he lost balance. He toppled backward into the fresh straw of the paddock with a thump and a cloud of dust. The dragonet pranced away, a scrap of Kai's tunic dangling from its jaws like a battle trophy.

"Emberstriker!" Kai shouted after the retreating dragonet. "That was my best shirt! Well, my only clean one anyway!"

"Stormwing, tell your cousin to pick on someone his own size," Pryce called toward the sky, unable to suppress his laughter. "Though I'd say the runt has good taste in targets."

6

Stormwing dove from the clouds. She skimmed the pen so low that Kai's already flattened hair stood straight up in her back draft.

"By the lake's depths!" Kai spit out straw. "Is everyone determined to annoy me today? Some friend you are, Stormwing!"

The storm dragon banked sharply upward, executing a perfect barrel roll that seemed to express her amusement.

Jorr sauntered over with a coil of freshly spliced rope draped across his shoulders. "Kai, if you'd stay upright for five minutes, the dragons might mistake you for an adult."

"Ha," Kai said from the straw, plucking golden stalks from his hair. "Comedy at my expense. Truly, Emberfall is paradise." He flopped back dramatically, spread-eagled. "Just leave me here to die of embarrassment."

"Die quietly then," Jorr said, uncoiling his rope. "Some of us have actual work to do."

"Work? Is that what we're calling Pryce's butchery of innocent lumber now?" Kai propped himself up on his elbows. "I thought we were running a dragon sanctuary, not a torture chamber for trees."

Pryce chuckled but kept carving—now fussing the dragon's jawline. The steady rhythm of gouge against wood had become almost meditative over the past weeks. The sanctuary was taking shape around them—rebuilt barns, expanded paddocks, the Swiftwind gradually becoming seaworthy again. It felt right, this place of healing for dragons and Shorlings alike.

"You know," Pryce said, stepping back to assess his work, "this might actually start looking like a proper dragon if you'd—"

A Tidewing gull interrupted with a piercing cry as it dive-bombed the worksite. It skidded to a halt beside Pryce's boot, sending wood chips flying. It stuck out a banded leg bearing a brass message capsule.

"Faye's messenger service grows more dramatic by the day," Kai said, finally picking himself up from the straw. "That bird looked at me like I owe it money."

"You probably do," Jorr said. "Birds have long memories, especially for debt."

Pryce rolled his eyes at their banter as he carefully unlaced the tiny capsule. Inside, three hurried lines from Faye leapt off the small piece of vellum:

RAID ON SHELTER COVE. BLACK SAILS. NAVY STILL ABSENT. COME.

The light mood evaporated instantly. Stormwing must have sensed the change; she landed behind Pryce with a ground-shaking thud, her wings creating a gust that sent wood shavings swirling like snow.

Kai dusted straw from his sleeves. "Bad news?"

"Shelter Cove's been raided by ships with black sails. I think Corsairs have ships like that," Pryce said. "They want me back at the mainland."

"Shelter Cove?" Jorr said, alarmed. "That's less than half a day's sail from Crystal Shores."

Jorr swore in Dragonkin—curses that sounded like ancient prophecy. "Volunteers won't stop them. Not without the navy backing them."

"How many families live in Shelter Cove?" Kai asked.

"Twenty, maybe thirty," Pryce said. "Mostly fishermen and their families." He shoved his tools into a roll.

He whistled, and Ash came darting from the stables, the gray cat leaping onto a fence post. Skye circled once overhead before landing beside her message-bearing companion. The animals had followed Pryce from Crystal Shores to Emberfall and back countless times since the battle, loyal beyond explanation.

"Stay with Jorr," Pryce told them, giving Ash a quick scratch behind the ears. The cat yowled in protest but settled on his perch, tail swishing in disapproval.

Pryce slung his bow across his back and secured his quiver of arrows at his hip. He vaulted to Stormwing's shoulder, the leather saddle creaking as he settled into position. The bow's curved limb pressed against his spine.

Kai grabbed a spear from the rack beside the barn. "I'm coming. Someone has to keep you from noble, heroic stupidity."

"Like charging into burning buildings?" Pryce raised an eyebrow. "Or was it facing down Dragonkin warriors with nothing but a kitchen knife that time in Rushwater?"

"Those were calculated risks," Kai said, approaching Stormwing. "Besides, you're one to talk. 'Oh look, a massive storm dragon is falling from the sky. Let me just run over and introduce myself, shall I?'"

"That worked out pretty well, wouldn't you say?" Pryce patted Stormwing's neck, earning a rumble of agreement from the beast.

"Statistically, that shouldn't have worked," Kai said.

Stormwing bumped Kai's hip with her snout—just hard enough to shove him onto the saddle behind Pryce. Kai grabbed Pryce's shoulders with undignified haste.

"Easy!" Kai said. "Can't you teach your overgrown lightning bolt some manners?"

"She has manners," Pryce said, securing the riding straps. "She just doesn't waste them on you."

Jorr stepped back, raising a hand in farewell. "I'll keep things running here. Don't do anything reckless."

"Us? Reckless?" Kai's laugh held a nervous edge. "Perish the thought."

The dragon gathered herself, and with a thunderous beat of her wings, she leapt skyward.

"Gods and little fishes!" Kai shouted over the wind. "A little warning next time!"

Emberfall's whitewashed barns dwindled below, the half-rebuilt sanctuary growing smaller with each powerful wing stroke. Pryce's unfinished dragon figurehead—that hopeful symbol of their peaceful new life—was just a speck now, fading into the distance as they soared toward a darker reality.

***

They touched down near Crystal Shores' main pier before the sun's shadow reached noonbell. Pryce dismounted into organized chaos: nets abandoned in tangled heaps, barrels overturned and leaking their contents across the dock, villagers clustering around Harbormaster Westley as if he could sprout cannons from his beard by sheer force of their collective will.

"Move those barrels!" Westley bellowed at a group of fishermen. "If one spark hits that lamp oil, we'll have our own fire to worry about!"

Westley's spyglass ticked against his palm like an impatient metronome as he caught sight of Pryce. "About time you showed up, Harper-Green. Shelter Cove's in ashes. Black hulled brigantines—fast ones. They struck before dawn and vanished west."

11

"Casualties?" Pryce asked, dreading the answer.

"Unknown. We've got refugees coming in by wagon. Some say half the village was still burning when they fled."

Old Man Finnegan limped up with his walking cane. "Told 'em decades ago: 'When the lake goes quiet, keep an ear for the whisper that follows.' Nobody listens to an old dragon hunter until the flames are dancing on their doorstep."

"We're listening now, Finnegan," Pryce said. "Did you see their approach?"

"Pah!" Finnegan spat. "If I'd seen 'em, I'd have sent warning. But I felt 'em." He tapped his chest. "Lake's been too peaceful these past weeks. Too still. Like it's holding its breath."

"Poetic, but not helpful," Westley grumbled.

Stormwing, apparently bored with Shorling conversation, stretched her long neck to investigate Westley's brass telescope. She sniffed it curiously, then sneezed a bolt of harmless static that made the metal ping! like a triangle chime. Westley jumped back, nearly falling.

"Confounded beast! That's precision equipment!"

Kai laughed, finally finding his land legs after the flight. "She approves your instrument, Harbor master. Consider yourself honored." He bowed with exaggerated formality. "The great Stormwing

12

doesn't bestow her lightning sneezes on just anyone."

"Lightning sneezes," Westley said, wiping soot from the lens with a corner of his jacket. "As if regular dragons weren't trouble enough." Despite his gruff tone, he gave Stormwing a respectful nod before turning to Pryce. "Mayor's summoned emergency council. You're late already and not even there yet."

"Not fashionably late?" Kai asked innocently.

"About as fashionable as those pitch stains on your trousers," Westley said, pointing to the dark smears on Kai's clothing—souvenirs from their ongoing repairs to the Swiftwind's hull.

"These?" Kai looked down at his pants. "These are the very latest in nautical couture, I'll have you know. All the best sailors are wearing tar this season."

"Save it for someone who cares, Frostborne," Westley said. "Council Hall. Now."

In Council Hall, bodies packed the chamber. Voices competed in a rising tide of fear.

"Order!" Mayor Wright shouted, her gavel striking the podium. "Shelter Cove has two trawlers with burned rigging, one family missing, and we have no war fleet." She adjusted her spectacles and surveyed the room until her gaze settled on the youngest person present. "Mister Pryce Harper-Green?"

A murmur rippled through the chamber as all eyes turned to Pryce. He straightened, noting the streaks of pitch tar not only on Kai's clothing, but smeared across his own breeches from the morning's work beneath the Swiftwind's hull. "Yes, Mayor Wright?"

"That storm dragon of yours—Stormwing— she's swift and can travel undetected if needed, correct?" When Pryce nodded, she continued, "I know you're just eighteen years but I have a simple and crucial task for you. I need you to scout the western waters, locate these Corsairs if possible, and return immediately with their position and numbers. No engagement, young man—strictly observation. Can you do this?"

Pryce nodded again. "Stormwing and I can scout the lake, mark their routes. We'll find their ships and report back."

Councilor Markham stood, his substantial girth forcing several others to shuffle sideways. His mustache twitched like an agitated caterpillar. "All well and good, but the boy must exercise extreme caution. These aren't fishing boats he's tracking— they're armed raiders with long-range weapons. All I'm saying is that Pryce needs to be absolutely sure he's not seen, for his safety and ours. A dragon in the sky could provoke them to attack sooner rather than later."

Kai stepped forward, spear in hand. "Better to see them coming than to sit blind, waiting for black sails to appear on our doorstep."

"And who asked you, Frostborne?" Markham's face reddened. "This isn't some game for children to play at being scouts. If they spot that dragon, they'll know we're onto them. If they capture the Harper-Green boy, they could extract information about our defenses—what little we have."

"Enough," Mayor Wright said before Kai could respond. "Mister Harper-Green, do you understand your mission? Scout only, locate their position, and return to Crystal Shores with all possible speed. No heroics, no confrontation."

"I understand, Mayor.".

Tyler Harper-Green rose from his council seat. "Mayor Wright, while my son is scouting, we should prepare defenses. These corsairs struck Shelter Cove with precision—they'll do the same to us if we're not ready."

"What do you suggest, Councilor?" the mayor asked.

Tyler moved to the large map of Crystal Shores spread across the table. "We need patrols in the water—Finnegan, Tobias, and whoever else can sail. We should string lantern buoys in the narrows as warning signals, rig spiked rafts at the breakwater to damage their hulls, and post lookouts with Faye's messenger gulls on rotation."

"And where do you propose we find the men for these patrols?" Markham said, tugging at his collar in agitation. "Our able bodies are already stretched thin with reconstruction, and let's not forget our Oceanrider fleet is still at Port Ravenspur, being repaired after the Dragonkin attack six months ago. All we have is a single navy vessel—the Tempest Guardian—and she's hardly enough to patrol our entire coastline."

"The Oceanriders left a contingent behind," Tyler countered, placing his hands on the map table. "Captain Henley may have taken the main fleet for repairs, but he's not a fool. There are at least two dozen trained Oceanriders still stationed here in Crystal Shores—men and women who know these waters better than any Corsair."

"Two dozen against how many raiders?" Markham scoffed.

"Two dozen trained fighters who can organize the volunteers," Tyler said. "Corrin's been maintaining a skeleton crew for the Tempest Guardian. They've been drilling the younger folk in basic defense tactics. And my old friend Declan has been staying with us—he served three campaigns against Corsairs before becoming a cook."

"A cook?" Markham's mustache bristled. "We're relying on cooks and volunteers now?"

"We're relying on everyone with skills to contribute," Tyler said. "Those who can't patrol can build defenses. Old Doyle's goats can't pull nets, but

16

they can haul timber for barricades. The women can prepare fire arrows and pitch bombs."

Pryce watched his father with admiration. He'd seen Tyler on fishing boats and at home, but rarely in his role as councilor.

Finnegan rapped his stick against the floor, the sound like a cannon shot. "Hope rows the boat, lads, but a spear keeps the shark from climbing aboard. Tyler's right. We use what we have, or we lose what we love."

A momentary silence followed his words. Then Tobias Underhill cleared his throat. "My trading vessel can be outfitted for patrol by evening tide. It's not much, but it's fast."

"Rusty Anchor Inn will provide food for the volunteers," Brim added from the back.

"I can organize the messenger birds," Faye piped up from where she stood near the door, her red curls bouncing as she moved forward. "We've expanded the network since the battle. We can have warnings to all coastal villages within hours."

Murmurs of reluctant approval spread through the chamber. The mayor exhaled. "Motion carried. Get to work before those raiders fancy Crystal Shores for their next trophy run."

After several hours of debate, the council adjourned in a scrape of chairs against worn floorboards. The chamber emptied quickly, villagers hurrying to their assigned tasks.

Outside, Pryce paused beneath a swaying lantern, staring toward the distant silhouette of the Island of Emberfall where his half carved dragon figurehead waited.

Stormwing crouched beside him. Pryce rested his forehead against her warm scales. "Think we can scare off a few puny Corsairs? Show them what happens when they mess with us?"

Stormwing huffed, and nudged him with enough force to make him stagger. The message was clear: *Stop doubting and start doing.*

"Right, no more brooding," Pryce agreed, patting her neck. "Time to remind these raiders why Crystal Shores is still standing after everything else that's tried to destroy it."

"If you're done sweet-talking your dragon," Kai called, approaching with a bundle of supplies, "some of us would like to get this patrol started before we're all old and gray. Or in Finnegan's case, older and grayer."

"I heard that," Finnegan called from where he was organizing a group of reluctant-looking fishermen. "Keep talking, and I'll have you scrubbing barnacles off every hull in the harbor!"

"You and what army?" Kai shot back, grinning. "Last I checked, you need both hands just to keep that walking stick upright!"

Finnegan brandished his walking stick, shaking it in Kai's direction, amused.

"This old sea dog still has enough bite left to teach you some manners. I was tanning hides and scraping hulls when your father was still learning to tie his first knot."

Pryce smiled. Some things never changed, even with Corsairs on the horizon.

Kai clambered up behind him on Stormwing's back, still griping about saddle pins and potential death. "If we die, I'm haunting you for eternity," he said, securing his spear to the saddle. "And I'll be the most annoying ghost you've ever encountered."

"You're already the most annoying living person I've encountered. How much worse could your ghost be?"

"Oh, you have no idea. I'd move your tools when you weren't looking. Hide your boots. Make mysterious noises during important conversations."

"So, exactly what you do now?"

"But *spookier*."

Finnegan pointed westward—toward where the raiders had vanished after their attack on Shelter Cove. "Keep your eyes sharp and your wits sharper! And don't do anything I wouldn't do!"

"That leaves us a surprisingly wide range of options," Kai said.

Stormwing launched skyward with a powerful thrust of her wings, the sudden acceleration forcing a yelp from Kai.

It looked peaceful from this height, in the way a sleeping giant sometimes looks peaceful before it wakes hungry for destruction. But this was their home, and they would defend it—dragons, gulls, goats, and all.

CHAPTER 2

Stormwing soared through the twilight. Crystal Shores shrank to a ragged necklace of lantern pearls below them, then even those vanished.

"Higher," Pryce shouted.

The dragon clawed for altitude until wind hissed through the saddle rings.

Behind him, Kai clung to the rear cantle, his spear butt thumping against Pryce's boot with each of Stormwing's powerful wing strokes.

"If you grip any tighter, you'll leave permanent dents in the saddle leather," Pryce called back to Kai.

"I'm securing myself properly. Unlike some reckless dragon-riders who think the sky is just another fishing boat deck."

Pryce glanced back at his white-knuckled friend. "You were braver back on the ground when you volunteered for this."

"Bravery looks different from a thousand feet up," Kai shouted as they hit a pocket of turbulent air. "If I fall, just make sure they carve something heroic on my marker stone instead of 'died screaming like a frightened child.'"

Lake Dragontide stretched below them. Thirty miles west lay Shelter Cove's smoking timbers—and somewhere beyond, the raiders who had kindled them.

"See anything?" Kai shouted.

Pryce lifted Finnegan's spyglass. Moonlight spilled across the lens. He swept north to south until a shadow broke the seam of water and sky.

"There!" He nudged Stormwing's left shoulder with a gentle boot heel, their practiced signal for turning. The dragon banked.

Ahead, three long, flat warships sailed with black canvas. Their wooden sides were painted black. The dim orange glow from covered fire-pots lit the ships with eerie light. Between them floated a wide, heavy boat filled with metal cages that made Pryce think of how the Dragonkin once carried their captured dragons.

Kai whistled low through his teeth. "Corsair animal pen. They're not just raiders—they're beast-tamers."

A ripple spread across the lake's surface. Pryce's stomach turned as he spotted the seadrake: a long shape of dark scales cutting through the water, bigger than two fishing boats put together. A chain of heavy iron links stretched from the back of the ship to a thick collar locked around the beast's neck.

The seadrake's existence confirmed Pryce's suspicions—these weren't ordinary raiders. Only the Corsairs had mastered the dark art of binding seadrakes to their will.

Pryce steadied the glass, focusing on the ships' details. Lantern code winked on the rearmost ship— three short flashes, one long—signaling westward into the darkness. Beyond the fleet, almost invisible against the black-on-black horizon, pinpricks of answering light suggested a second wave of vessels.

"They're calling reinforcements," Pryce said. "This isn't a raid—it's an invasion force."

"That's our cue to leave," Kai said, his fingers digging into Pryce's shoulders. "We've seen more than enough, and Mayor Wright specifically said 'no heroics.'"

Pryce nodded and guided Stormwing closer, wanting one final look at the Corsair weapons before returning to Crystal Shores. It was a mistake. As they banked around the trailing ship, Stormwing's silhouette caught the moonlight.

"Pryce!" Kai shouted. "We've got company below!"

Two Corsair lookouts on the mainmast had spotted them; one pointed upward, shouting to his companions while the other reached for his weapon. Moonlight glinted off a raised crossbow as it swung in their direction.

"Hang on!"

Pryce leaned forward, pressing himself against Stormwing's neck, and shouted, "Fly."

Stormwing folded her wings and dove with the sudden grace of a hunting falcon. Air howled past them, watering his eyes. Bolts hissed overhead, one striking a trailing rein with a metallic *twang* that vibrated through the saddle.

"That was too close!" Kai shouted.

Before the Corsair gunners could reload, Stormwing skimmed the wave tops, her talons spraying silver arcs through the black water. Kai whooped in terrified exhilaration as they sped away from the ships. "Like outrunning a hurricane on the back of the storm itself!"

They headed south, using the island shadows to mask their retreat. Only then did Pryce let Stormwing ease into a glide. The dragon's sides heaved beneath him, her breath coming in great gusts.

"I've seen enough Corsair hospitality to last several lifetimes," Kai said, still holding on for dear life.

A light bobbed ahead on the dark lake. Pryce signaled Stormwing to slow her flight. As they drew closer, he could make out a fishing skiff with its sail torn to shreds, one side charred black from fire. Two more fishing boats drifted nearby, lashed together and packed with villagers.

Pryce guided Stormwing lower, her wing-beats sending gentle ripples across the water's surface.

"We're from Crystal Shores," he called down.

A gray-haired matron waved up at them, her voice ragged with exhaustion and smoke. "They burned everything! Five families didn't make it to the boats."

These weren't just refugees—they were the first casualties in a war Crystal Shores wasn't prepared to fight.

From the closest boat, a thick Corsair boarding rope still hung over the side, its metal hook caught deep in the splintered wood.

"Head east to the village," Pryce instructed the refugees, pointing toward Crystal Shores. "Follow the lighthouse beam—they'll be watching for survivors. Go quickly!"

As Stormwing wheeled skyward once more, Pryce noticed another glimmer—this one moving across open water. A lone Corsair scout-vessel headed west, lantern code flashing briskly from its bow. The pattern was different from what they'd seen earlier—more urgent, perhaps carrying news of refugee sightings or even their own dragon-backed surveillance.

"I think they're calling reinforcements," Pryce said.

Without warning, a black-feathered arrow lanced upward from the scout boat, arcing toward them. Stormwing rolled instinctively. The arrow's head exploded in a puff of stinging ash—Corsair flashpowder meant to illuminate targets for archers below.

"The next one might burn," Kai said, brushing ash from his sleeve. "Time to disappear."

Stormwing needed no further encouragement. She climbed into a bank of clouds. Hidden in the mist, they hovered while Pryce considered their options.

"We can't lead them straight back to Crystal Shores," he said. "They'll track our flight path."

"So what's the plan?"

"We head north first, toward Thunder Peaks," Pryce said. "Then east along the ridge line, and finally south to Crystal Shores. It'll take longer, but we'll throw off any trackers."

"Assuming we don't freeze to death first."

The detour added hours to their journey. They skimmed the choppy waters of North Channel, where the lake narrowed between sheer cliffs. Twice they spotted Corsair scout vessels and had to hide in cloud cover, holding position until the danger passed. Stormwing's breathing grew increasingly labored, her wing beats becoming shallow and forced.

"She can't keep this up much longer," Kai said as they finally turned southeast. The Thunder Peaks were far behind them now.

"Just a bit further," Pryce encouraged, stroking Stormwing's neck. He could feel the exhaustion in her muscles.

By the time they crossed into Crystal Shores' waters, the night had passed. Stars had faded from the eastern sky and the first pale gray light of dawn lightened the sky. Pryce's eyes burned with fatigue as he scanned the horizon, alert for any sign of pursuing vessels.

"There!" Kai pointed ahead to the Crystal Shores' lighthouse.

Stormwing alighted on the bluff's grassy brim, exhausted.

Kai dismounted first and promptly bent double, hands braced on his knees. "If we never do that again. I'll die content."

Pryce slid down from the saddle. His legs felt like rubber. He unclenched his fist; Finnegan's spyglass was still there. His fingers had cramped around it during their long flight, and now they ached as he tucked it carefully into his belt.

"Stormwing needs rest," he said, stroking the dragon's neck as she settled onto her haunches, wings folded tightly against her sides. "I pushed her too hard."

Stormwing's eyes drooped, her massive sides heaving with each breath.

"Go," Pryce said to her. "Find somewhere quiet to recover."

Stormwing dragged herself toward a sheltered alcove near the lighthouse keeper's cottage. She circled three times before collapsing into an exhausted heap, her tail curling protectively around her body.

"Will she be all right?" Kai asked.

"She needs time," Pryce said. "Something we don't have much of."

From the village below came the toll of the warning bell—three sharp rings followed by one long peal. The emergency council summons.

"They're waiting," Kai said, nodding toward the town hall.

"Let's go," Pryce said.

As they descended the bluff path toward the village, the first boats were already pushing off from the docks—fishermen heading out not for their morning catch, but to serve as the first wave of lookouts.

Pryce had told himself the Dragonkin attack six months ago would be the last battle Crystal Shores ever faced—at least for a long time.

Now he knew better.

"You look like that giant's about to wake," Kai said, elbowing him gently.

"It is." Pryce looked ahead at the council hall, where he would have to tell his neighbors, his friends, his family exactly what danger sailed toward their shores.

CHAPTER 3

The council chamber buzzed with tension. Pryce stood near the back wall, his shoulders aching from the long flight. Beside him, Kai slouched against a support beam.

Mayor Wright took her place at the podium, gavel in hand. Unlike yesterday's emergency meeting, today every seat was filled—fishermen in stained clothing, merchants in their finest attire, and mothers with worry on their faces.

"This council is now in session," Mayor Wright announced. "As you all know, Shelter Cove lies in ruins. Thanks to Pryce and Kai's reconnaissance, we know the threat we face."

Pryce moved forward when called upon, conscious of the lingering scent of dragon scales that clung to his clothing.

"Three brigantines, heavily armed. An auxiliary barge with metal cages." He swallowed hard. "And a seadrake, chained but controlled. They have lantern signals to the west—likely more ships coming. This isn't a random raid; it's organized. Military."

A wave of murmurs swept through the hall. Someone toward the back began to sob.

"What about Stormwing?" Old Man Finnegan called from his seat in the front row. "How's she faring after the flight?"

"Exhausted. She needs rest."

"Then our air advantage is temporarily grounded," Tyler said. "We need to focus on sea and shore defenses until she recovers."

Councilor Markham heaved his substantial frame from his chair, mustache bristling. "What we *need* is the Oceanrider fleet! One vessel—the Tempest Guardian—against three brigantines? It's suicide!"

"The main fleet won't return from Port Ravenspur for at least five days," Tyler said. "We work with what we have."

"Which is nothing!" Markham said. "A few fishing boats, some nets, and a half-repaired naval vessel. The Corsairs will burn us like they burned Shelter Cove!"

Tobias Underhill rose next, his merchant's cap clutched in his hands. "We've placed lantern buoys at the narrows and prepared the spiked rafts for the breakwater. My trading vessel has been outfitted with ballistae—crude, but functional."

"And the lookout posts?" Mayor Wright asked.

"Manned and ready," Ana called from where she stood by the door, a sword at her hip. "We've got rotations scheduled for the next three days, signaling protocols established."

Tyler nodded approvingly. "Helmsman Brock has the Tempest Guardian ready with a skeleton crew. It's not much, but positioned correctly, she can protect our harbor entrance."

"What about evacuations?" asked a woman holding a sleeping infant.

"The inland caves are prepared," Faye said. Her red curls were tied back in a braid. "We've stocked supplies for three days. Messenger birds are positioned for emergency alerts."

Mayor Wright adjusted her spectacles. "Good. Now we need to—"

The council chamber doors burst open. A young boy, no more than twelve, stumbled in, wide-eyed and breathless.

"Ship!" he gasped. "Coming from the east!"

"East?" Tyler's head snapped up. "The Corsairs were headed west."

"It's flying a strange silver flag!" the boy said, panting hard from his run. "With golden dragons on it!"

"It's the Dragonkin's sign of parley," Finnegan said. "They're requesting a meeting—want to talk terms without bloodshed."

The chamber erupted in chaos.

31

"Dragonkin!" Markham slammed his fist on the table. "As if one enemy weren't enough!"

"Not here for shore leave, that's certain," Finnegan said, leaning on his walking stick.

"Everyone remain calm," Mayor Wright said, pounding her gavel as Harbormaster Westley entered the chamber. "Let's assess before we panic. Harbormaster Westley, what do you know?"

Westley stood by the door, his brass spyglass clutched in one hand. "Single ship approaching the eastern pier. Flying truce flags. They're requesting permission to dock under diplomatic protocol."

"Deny them!" Markham said. "We barely survived their last attack!"

"That was six months ago," Tyler reminded him. "And they withdrew after Pryce negotiated the truce."

"Negotiated?" Markham said. "The boy got lucky with the princess liking him, nothing more."

"Enough, Councilor. The Dragonkin ship flies truce flags. We will honor diplomatic protocol." She turned to Westley. "Grant them permission to dock. Escort their envoy—and *only* their envoy—to Council Hall."

As the harbormaster departed, Markham huffed and puffed in his seat. "Mark my words, they're here to finish what they started. First the Dragonkin attack, then the Corsairs just *happen* to invade? Too convenient!"

"Coincidence doesn't equal conspiracy," Tobias said. "Let's hear what they have to say."

An uncomfortable silence fell over the chamber.

The wait stretched like salt taffy, minutes becoming an hour. Outside, they could hear the distant commotion of the Dragonkin vessel docking, the shouted commands of Westley's harbor guards, the shouts of frightened villagers.

When the doors finally opened again, Harbormaster Westley entered first, followed by a towering figure cloaked in midnight blue. The Dragonkin stood nearly a head and a half taller than the Shorling guards flanking him, his broad shoulders and imposing frame making the villagers appear childlike by comparison. For one terrible moment, Pryce thought Queen Nymeria herself had come—but as the hood fell back, he saw it was another Dragonkin altogether.

The elderly envoy's face bore the hallmarks of his race—deep indigo scales covered most of his visible skin, not merely at his temples like Seren's, but extending down his neck and across his cheekbones in ridged patterns. His eyes, larger than a Shorling's, surveyed the room with predatory calculation. When he spoke, his lips pulled back to reveal teeth that came to subtle points, not filed like some Dragonkin, but naturally shaped for tearing.

"I bring greetings from Queen Nymeria of the Dragonkin realm." His voice carried the subtle resonance characteristic of those born to the Dragonkin bloodlines, deeper and more powerful than seemed natural. "I am Commander Shadowspear, emissary to Her Majesty."

Mayor Wright inclined her head formally. "Crystal Shores acknowledges your diplomatic status, Commander. State your business."

Shadowspear surveyed the room, his gaze lingering on Pryce for a moment longer than comfortable.

"Queen Nymeria offers an alliance," he said simply.

Disbelief rippled through the chamber.

"An alliance?" Markham said. "With the same Dragonkin who tried to burn our village to the ground?"

"The queen acknowledges past . . . misunderstandings. But now we face a common enemy. The Corsairs threaten both Dragonkin and Shorling territories."

"So they've attacked you as well?" Tyler asked, arms crossed.

"Three outposts along our eastern shores have been raided. Their fleet grows bolder." Shadowspear reached into his cloak and produced a scroll sealed with crimson wax. "The terms of our proposed alliance are detailed here. Queen Nymeria offers immediate military assistance—five warships, three aerial dragon squadrons, and ground forces sufficient to defend your shores."

Markham seemed momentarily silenced by the scale of the offered aid.

"And what does Queen Nymeria want in return?" Mayor Wright asked, not reaching for the scroll.

Shadowspear's eyes found Pryce again. "A formal alliance between our peoples, sealed in the traditional manner—through marriage."

Silence gripped the chamber.

"Marriage?" Tyler asked. "Between whom, exactly?"

"Princess Seren, daughter of Queen Nymeria, and—" Shadowspear paused, pointing one scaled finger directly at Pryce, "—the dragon trainer of Crystal Shores."

Chaos erupted. Markham leapt to his feet, face purple with rage. Councilors shouted over one another.

"Absolutely not!" Finnegan slammed his walking stick against the floor. "The boy's barely eighteen!"

"Princess Seren is of comparable age," Shadowspear replied coolly. "The union would symbolize lasting peace between our peoples."

"Peace?" Markham laughed. "Is that what you call forcing a boy into marriage with one of your scaled monstrosities?"

Shadowspear's eyes flashed. "Careful, Councilor. Her Highness is of royal blood—dragon blood. The same blood that flows, albeit diluted, in young Harper-Green's veins."

Pryce felt eyes turn toward him—not questioning, but protective of one of their own despite the scales still visible along his jawline from the Dragonkin's previous conversion attempt.

"We know our son's heritage," Ellie said. "What does that have to do with these attacks?"

"Ah, but do you know what it truly means, madame?" Shadowspear said. "The ancient bloodlines still sing in his veins. We recognize our own, even when diluted by . . . other lineages. And that makes him valuable—perhaps more valuable than this quaint fishing village realizes."

Tyler shifted closer to his son, a subtle movement that didn't escape Shadowspear's notice.

"The question isn't what we know," Tyler said. "It's what you want."

Mayor Wright banged her gavel repeatedly until order was restored. "This proposal requires careful consideration. The council will—"

"There is no time for deliberation," Shadowspear interrupted. "The Corsair fleet approaches your western shore even now. Our ships and dragons stand ready, but we require an answer before sundown."

Tyler clenched his fists. "This is coercion, not diplomacy."

"This is survival," Shadowspear countered. "For both our peoples."

A messenger burst into the chamber, sweat streaming down his face. He hurried to Mayor Wright, whispering urgently in her ear; the news clearly affecting her.

"What is it?" Councilor Markham asked.

"Three more fishing vessels found abandoned near the North Channel," she said. "No survivors, but . . ." She swallowed hard. "Corsair weapons left behind. And something else—scales from a bound seadrake. They're testing our defenses."

The room erupted in frightened chaos. Finnegan's walking stick struck the floor three times, commanding silence.

"They're mapping our response times," he said. "Seeing how quickly we react to distress calls before their main force arrives."

Shadowspear's expression remained impassive. "The terms of our alliance stand. Decide quickly, or decide alone."

In that crushing quiet, a second messenger entered, this one carrying a sealed dispatch with the Oceanrider insignia. He approached Tyler and Ellie.

"Urgent summons from Captain Henley," the messenger said. "You're both needed at Port Ravenspur immediately. Diplomatic emergency."

Tyler broke the seal, his eyes scanning the message. He exchanged a look with Ellie.

"We have to go," he said reluctantly. "Henley wouldn't call us both unless it was critical."

"Now?" Pryce asked. "With Corsairs approaching and—" he glanced at Shadowspear, "—this marriage proposal?"

Councilor Markham slammed his palm on the table. "This is preposterous! Our defenses hanging by a thread, and now our most experienced council members summoned away? It reeks of sabotage."

"Mind your accusations, Councilor," Shadowspear said. "The Dragonkin offer protection, not subterfuge. Without us, Crystal Shores might become nothing more than cinders and memory."

Mayor Wright raised her hands for silence. "What exactly does this engagement entail? How soon? What guarantees does Crystal Shores receive?"

"Princess Seren would arrive to formalize the arrangement. The betrothal period would last one month, during which our combined forces would defend against the Corsair threat. Upon marriage, Crystal Shores would fall under Dragonkin protection permanently."

Tyler set the message down and turned to Pryce. "I don't like this timing any more than you do. But Henley's message mentions movement among the northern tribes. If they're forming alliances with the Corsairs . . ."

"We'd be facing attacks from multiple fronts," Ellie finished.

Tyler nodded before addressing the council. "In my absence, I hereby appoint my son, Pryce

Harper-Green, as acting councilor with full authority to represent our family's interests. Do any present object to this appointment?"

The room remained silent. Even Markham, despite his scowl, offered no challenge.

Tyler turned back to Pryce, speaking quietly but with intensity. "This isn't how I imagined passing the mantle, son."

"What about the Dragonkin proposal?" Pryce asked. "Do you really think I should—"

"I think," Tyler said, "that sometimes we must make impossible choices to protect what matters most. Your mother and I had to make such choices once. Now it's your turn."

"Shadowspear," Ellie said, "what guarantees do we have that you won't simply seize what you want once this alliance is formalized? Your reputation isn't built on honesty."

Shadowspear inclined his head slightly. "Skepticism is expected, Madame. But consider this: the Corsairs threaten both our peoples. We offer legitimate protection through ancient custom— marriage has sealed alliances for millennia. Our intentions are . . . transparent."

"Transparent as morning fog," Finnegan said.

Mayor Wright pressed her fingertips to her temples. "We're running out of options and time."

All eyes turned to Pryce.

"I'll do it," he said. "I'll agree to the engagement."

"Pryce, no!" Kai pushed away from the wall where he'd been watching in shocked silence.

"We need their ships and dragons," Pryce said. "An engagement isn't a marriage. It buys us time."

"Smart boy." Shadowspear grinned.

Ellie crossed to her son. "You don't have to do this. We'll find another way."

"There is no other way. Not in time."

Mayor Wright surveyed the room. "Then it's settled. Crystal Shores provisionally accepts the terms of alliance, pending formal approval by the full council."

"The queen will be pleased," Shadowspear said, a hint of satisfaction in his voice. "Princess Seren will arrive tomorrow to formalize the engagement."

Markham muttered something under his breath.

As the council adjourned, Kai approached Pryce. "You've lost your mind. Trading yourself to the Dragonkin?"

"I'm buying us time. And ships. And dragons."

"At what cost?"

Before Pryce could answer, his parents approached.

Ellie pulled him into an embrace. "We'll be back as soon as possible. Don't let them push you into anything more than an engagement. *Nothing* is final until we return."

"I know, Mom."

Tyler clapped a hand on his shoulder. "Trust Finnegan and Tobias. They've seen more politics than most."

"And remember," Ellie added, "your blood is your own. Dragon or Shorling—it doesn't matter. *You* decide what it means."

Within the hour, his parents had departed on the fastest available skiff, bound for Port Ravenspur.

"Tell me I didn't just make a terrible mistake," Pryce said, turning to Kai.

"I'd love to, but I try not to lie to my friends." Kai raised an eyebrow.

"Thanks. Very helpful."

CHAPTER 4

Pryce stood at the edge of Crystal Shores' main dock. He felt uncomfortable in the stiff formal vest and high-collared shirt Mayor Wright had insisted he wear for the occasion. His usual fishing clothes had been deemed unacceptable for greeting a foreign dignitary—especially one he was now reluctantly "engaged" to.

"Stop fidgeting," Harbormaster Westley said beside him, his brass spyglass tapping rhythmically against his palm. "Makes you look nervous."

"I *am* nervous." Pryce tugged at his collar.

"Well, don't *look* it," Westley said, raising his spyglass to scan the horizon again. "Here they come. Right on time, I'll give them that."

In the distance, a sleek vessel approached through the morning mist. Unlike the old fishing boats that filled Crystal Shores' harbor, the Dragonkin ship cut through the water with precision, its crimson sails with golden thread caught the dawn light. At its prow, a carved dragon figurehead put Pryce's unfinished carving work at Emberfall to shame—the wooden creature seemed almost alive, its scales detailed down to individual ridges.

Mayor Wright cleared her throat, adjusting her ceremonial sash. "Remember, Pryce, we're playing for time. The Oceanrider fleet won't be back from Port Ravenspur for at least another week. Until then, this alliance is our best protection against those Corsairs you spotted."

"I understand."

"Chin up, lad," Old Man Finnegan said, appearing at Pryce's side with surprising quietness for someone who relied on a walking stick. "Remember what I taught you about dragons— show fear, and they'll smell it. Show strength, and they might just respect you."

"These aren't exactly dragons, Finnegan," Pryce said.

"Aren't they?" Finnegan raised a bushy eyebrow. "Part dragon, part Shorling, all trouble. Just like that beautiful beast of yours."

At the mention of Stormwing, Pryce glanced toward the hills where his dragon had been asked to stay. The storm dragon's presence might have been seen as threatening—or worse, as a challenge—to the Dragonkin delegation.

Kai approached from behind. "The villagers are gathering. Not all of them look happy about this."

Pryce turned to see a crowd forming along the waterfront. Children pushed to the front, eager for a glimpse of the legendary Dragonkin, while adults hung back, their expressions ranging from curious to openly hostile. Gordan Flintjaw stood with arms crossed, flanked by a group of burly fishermen who talked among themselves, occasionally spitting onto the ground in a clear sign of disrespect.

"Can't blame them," Kai said. "Six months isn't long enough to forget a war."

The Dragonkin vessel glided to a stop alongside the dock. Up close, the craftsmanship was even more impressive.

A gangplank extended from the ship with a soft thud against the wood of the dock. The crowd fell silent.

First came the honor guard—six Dragonkin warriors who dwarfed even the burliest fishermen of Crystal Shores. Their armor mimicked dragon scales, but beneath the metalwork, their actual scales were clearly visible on exposed forearms and necks.

Then she appeared.

Princess Seren stepped onto the gangplank with regal grace. Unlike her imposing guards, her form was more delicate, closer to Shorling proportions though still tall by Shorling standards. Her white dress flowed around her, its fabric adorned with silver threading. The subtle scales at her temples shifted from pale lavender to deeper purple as she moved. Her long blonde hair was partially braided with silver ornaments that clinked softly with each step.

But it was her violet eyes that caught Pryce's attention. When they landed on him, he felt a jolt of recognition, of memory—both pleasant and painful.

"The Princess Seren of the Dragonkin," announced a herald from the ship, his voice carrying across the suddenly silent harbor. "Daughter of Queen Nymeria, Keeper of the Eastern Flame, Ambassador of Drakemere Island."

Mayor Wright offered a formal bow. "Crystal Shores welcomes Princess Seren and her delegation. I am Mayor Helen Wright, and this—" she gestured to Pryce, "—is Pryce Harper-Green, acting council representative in his parents' absence."

Pryce drew closer, bowing stiffly as protocol demanded. When he straightened, he found Seren studying him.

"Crystal Shores is as quaint as you described it," Seren said, her voice carrying just enough to be heard by those closest.

"We find it suits us," Pryce said. "Though I imagine it lacks the grandeur you're accustomed to at Drakemere."

A hint of something—amusement? Approval?—crossed Seren's face before she composed herself again. "Formality suits you poorly, Pryce Harper-Green. But then, much has changed since we last met."

An uncomfortable silence fell between them, loaded with unspoken history. Mayor Wright cleared her throat.

"Perhaps we should proceed to the Great Hall for the formal welcome. The council is gathered, and refreshments have been prepared."

Seren nodded graciously. "Lead on, Mayor Wright. My guards will accompany us."

As the procession formed, Pryce found himself walking beside Seren, acutely aware of the stares from both villagers and Dragonkin guards.

"Your village still bears the scars of war," Seren said as they passed a building with scaffolding still attached.

"We rebuild quickly," Pryce said. "Shorlings are resilient."

"Indeed." Something softened in her expression. "I'm glad to see it recovering."

Before Pryce could respond, a clod of mud sailed through the air, barely missing Seren's shoulder. It splattered against the wall beside them. The Dragonkin guards immediately moved into defensive positions, hands going to weapons.

"Stand down!" Pryce ordered sharply, stepping between the guards and the crowd. He scanned the gathered faces, finding Gordan Flintjaw's sneering expression in the back. "We agreed to peace. That means *all* of us."

"Peace with dragon-lovers?" someone called from the crowd.

"Peace with those who can help us against the Corsairs," Pryce said. "Or would you rather face those black ships alone?"

A murmur ran through the crowd. The memory of Shelter Cove's destruction was still fresh, the fear of a similar fate for Crystal Shores very real.

"We proceed to the Great Hall," Mayor Wright announced. "Anyone disturbing the peace will answer to the council directly."

The procession continued, the mood even more strained. Kai fell into step beside Pryce.

"Well handled," he said. "Though I think you've made an enemy in Gordan."

"Gordan was already an enemy," Pryce replied under his breath. "He's just found a new excuse."

The Great Hall had been transformed for the occasion. Fresh garlands of local wildflowers hung from the rafters, their sweet scent mingling with the smokier aroma of ceremonial herbs burning in corner braziers. The long council table had been draped with Crystal Shores' finest linens— admittedly humble compared to Dragonkin standards, but the best they could offer.

Mayor Wright took her place at the head of the table, gesturing for Seren to sit at her right hand, with Pryce at her left. The remaining seats filled with council members and Dragonkin representatives, creating a checkerboard of divided loyalties. Councilor Markham's large body seemed to expand with indignation as he was seated beside a particularly scaled Dragonkin officer.

"Before we begin formal discussions," Mayor Wright said, "we offer refreshments in the tradition of Shorling hospitality."

Servers brought platters of local delicacies — smoked trout with wild herbs, freshwater crayfish in butter sauce, lake berry compote, and dark bread still warm from the oven. Simple fare, but the best Crystal Shores could produce.

Pryce noticed the subtle hesitation from the Dragonkin delegation as they regarded the unfamiliar food. Seren, to her credit, selected a piece of smoked trout and took a delicate bite, nodding appreciatively to Mayor Wright.

"Your lake produces excellent fish," she said. "Different from our sea varieties, but pleasant."

"We may have different customs," Mayor Wright replied, "but we share common enemies. The Corsairs you've heard about have already destroyed Shelter Cove, and our Oceanrider fleet remains at Port Ravenspur for repairs."

Councilor Markham set down his cup with deliberate force. "Curious how Corsairs attack just when Dragonkin need allies."

"Perhaps your renowned fishing expertise extends to fishing for trouble, Councilor," Seren said. "Though I assure you, the Dragonkin have no desire to see Shorling villages destroyed. It serves neither our interests nor yours."

"Fine words," Markham said. "But actions speak louder."

"Indeed they do," said one of the Dragonkin officers, his hand drifting toward the dagger at his belt. "Perhaps you'd care to see how *loud* Dragonkin actions can be?"

"Enough," Pryce said, his voice cracking. He felt the eyes of everyone at the table turn to him, and fought the urge to shrink back. "Councilor Markham, we . . . we agreed to host these guests with respect." His hands trembled on the table before he tucked them into his lap. "And," he continued, turning to the Dragonkin officer, "threats won't help us against the Corsairs."

Mayor Wright gave him an encouraging nod. "What Pryce means to say is that decorum must be maintained if this alliance is to succeed."

"You've changed since our last meeting, Pryce Harper-Green," Seren said.

"Not by choice," Pryce said, dropping his gaze. "My father always says when the storm comes, someone must steer the boat." He winced at how childish the reference to his father sounded in this formal setting.

"A quaint metaphor," said the Dragonkin officer with contempt. "Is this truly who speaks for Crystal Shores now? A boy hiding behind his father's sayings?"

Mayor Wright straightened in her chair. "Pryce Harper-Green represents his family's council seat with our full confidence, Commander. His age does not diminish his voice here."

Pryce thought his age *did* matter.

"Then let us discuss practical matters," the mayor said. "The terms of our alliance include joint patrols, shared intelligence, and . . ." she hesitated, "the formal engagement between Princess Seren and Pryce Harper-Green."

Several of the Dragonkin exchanged glances that Pryce couldn't interpret.

"These terms have been agreed upon," Seren said. "Though the formal ceremony will wait until my mother—Queen Nymeria—can attend."

The discussion turned to patrol schedules, watch positions, and communication protocols. Through it all, Pryce was acutely aware of Seren's presence.

As the meeting drew to a close, Mayor Wright suggested that Pryce show Seren the village's defenses while final arrangements were made for the Dragonkin quarters. It was clearly a diplomatic maneuver to give them time alone—time the mayor hoped would ease the obvious tension between the reluctant couple.

The afternoon sun cast long shadows across Crystal Shores as Pryce led Seren along the western battlement. Below them, villagers went about their business, though many stopped to stare at the Dragonkin princess.

"Your people don't trust me," Seren said.

"Can you blame them? The last time Dragonkin ships appeared in our waters, they came with fire and death."

"And now we come with offers of protection against a common enemy." Seren stopped, turning to face him. "This isn't how either of us imagined our futures, is it?"

The directness of the question caught Pryce off guard. "No. It's not."

For a moment, Seren's regal façade slipped, revealing something vulnerable beneath. "I never wanted—" she began, then stopped herself, glancing around to ensure they were truly alone. "Not everything was a lie, Pryce. Between us. Before."

"Words are easy," Pryce said. "Trust must be earned."

Her eyes held his for a long moment before she nodded. "Fair enough. I expect nothing less." She turned back to survey the village. "Your Stormwing—is she well?"

"She is." The question surprised him. "She's staying in the hills for now. I thought her presence might . . . complicate things."

"Wise," Seren agreed.

A Dragonkin guard approached, informing Seren that their quarters were prepared.

"Until tomorrow, then," Seren said, slipping back into her formal persona. "I look forward to our first joint patrol."

"Until tomorrow," Pryce echoed.

He watched her walk away. As she disappeared into the shadows of Crystal Shores' narrow streets, Pryce remained on the battlement.

Kai found him there some time later, as the first stars appeared in the eastern sky.

"Well?" his friend asked. "How was your royal tour?"

Pryce shook his head. "Complicated."

"She's pretty, I'll give her that," Kai said. "If you like the whole 'could kill you with a look' thing, which, apparently, you do."

Pryce smiled. "Thanks for the assessment."

Kai leaned against the battlement wall. "So, engaged to a Dragonkin princess. That should make for interesting family dinners."

"If we survive that long," Pryce said, his eyes drawn to the western horizon where the Corsair ships lurked.

"One day at a time," Kai said. "One very complicated, potentially deadly day at a time."

CHAPTER 5

Dawn broke over Crystal Shores. Pryce stood on the balcony of the Council Hall, watching as Dragonkin ships bobbed alongside Shorling fishing vessels in the harbor below. The strange alliance—forged in desperation and sealed with his own reluctant betrothal—had survived its first night, though not without incident. Twice he'd been summoned to break up arguments between Dragonkin guards and local fishermen.

He ran his fingers along the scales at his jawline—a permanent reminder of his connection to both worlds. Six months hadn't been enough time for the villagers to forget that the same scales marked those who had tried to burn Crystal Shores to the ground.

"You look like you've been awake all night," Kai said, appearing at his side with two steaming mugs. He handed one to Pryce. "Seaweed brew. Old Man Finnegan swears it cures everything from war wounds to broken hearts."

"And diplomatic disasters?" Pryce asked, accepting the mug.

"Probably not those." Kai leaned against the railing.

Below, a commotion erupted on the main pier as a Dragonkin vessel attempted to dock in a space traditionally reserved for Tobias's trading ship. Voices carried across the water, sharp with rising anger.

"And so it begins," Pryce sighed, setting down his mug. "First council meeting starts in an hour, and we're already fighting over dock space."

"Welcome to leadership," Kai said.

***

The Great Hall had been rearranged for the joint council meeting. The long table that normally dominated the center of the room had been replaced by two crescent-shaped tables facing each other across an open space. Mayor Wright had suggested the arrangement to avoid the appearance of one group sitting at the head of the table. Instead, Pryce occupied the center position of the Shorling crescent, directly facing Princess Seren at the center of the Dragonkin delegation.

"First item," Mayor Wright announced, "allocation of harbor space for our combined fleet."

Harbormaster Westley rose from his seat, unfurling a detailed map of Crystal Shores' harbor. "We have space for three Dragonkin vessels at the main pier," he said, tapping the parchment. "The remaining two will need to anchor in the deeper water here"—he pointed to the bay's eastern section—"and use small boats to ferry personnel."

"Unacceptable," said the Dragonkin naval commander, a broad-shouldered male with copper-colored scales. "Our warships require direct dock access for efficient deployment of troops and supplies."

"And our fishing boats require access to reach their daily grounds," Westley said. "Unless your warriors plan to eat their weapons, someone needs to bring in food."

"Perhaps," Pryce said, "we could establish a rotation. Three hours for fishing vessels in the morning, followed by Dragonkin access during military operations."

"And who decides what constitutes a military operation?" Councilor Markham said. "Are we to surrender our livelihoods at every Dragonkin whim?"

The Dragonkin commander started to rise, but Seren placed a restraining hand on his arm. "Councilor Markham raises a valid concern," she said. "Perhaps we need clearer definitions of operational priorities."

"I believe I can help with that," Kai said, approaching with a parchment of his own. Pryce shot him a questioning look—this wasn't part of any plan they'd discussed. "I've drafted a scheduling proposal based on tide patterns and typical fishing hours."

He spread the document on the table where both delegations could see. It detailed a complex system of harbor usage based on tide patterns, weather conditions, and military necessity.

"Where did this come from?" Pryce whispered as Kai returned to his position behind Pryce's chair.

"You're not the only one who's been preparing," Kai said.

After much discussion, a modified version of Kai's proposal was adopted, though neither side seemed entirely satisfied.

The second item on the agenda proved even more contentious: food rations.

"Our warriors require higher protein allocations than your fishing folk," stated a Dragonkin quartermaster, her silver-flecked scales catching the light as she consulted her own records. "Standard issue is two pounds of meat per soldier per day."

Tobias Underhill, who had been placed in charge of Crystal Shores' food inventory, choked on his drink. "Two pounds? Each? Daily?" He shook his head. "Impossible. Our current stores would be depleted within a week. Crystal Shores depends primarily on fish, not meat."

"Our warriors cannot fight on fish alone," the quartermaster said.

"Perhaps they should learn," Markham said, loud enough to be heard.

A Dragonkin sergeant—a burly male with jagged battle scars crossing the scales on his face— shot to his feet. "Typical Shorling ignorance. While you catch minnows in your little boats, we're preparing to save your miserable village."

Markham's face turned red. "We survived centuries before you scaled intruders appeared on our shores! And we were doing fine until—"

"Until the Corsairs started burning your villages," the Dragonkin sergeant finished. His hand moved to the hilt of his dagger. "Perhaps we should let them continue. One less Shorling settlement to worry about."

The hall erupted. Shorling councilors shouted over one another while Dragonkin representatives rose, hands moving to weapons. In the chaos, Pryce noticed Seren watching him.

Pryce stood, his palms damp with sweat as he tried to speak, but his voice came out as barely more than a croak. No one noticed. The chamber roared with arguing voices while Mayor Wright pounded her gavel.

"I—" he started again, but Councilor Markham's booming accusations drowned him out completely. Pryce's face flushed with embarrassment.

He slammed his fist on the table, wincing at the unexpected pain. "Quiet, please!" He managed, louder this time, but still insufficient. A few nearby heads turned, only to dismiss him with quick glances before returning to their heated debates.

Mayor Wright caught his eye and gave a small nod of encouragement. Pryce took a deep breath, then grabbed a metal cup and brought it down hard on the wooden table with a sharp *crack*.

"ENOUGH!" This time, about half the room paused, creating pockets of awkward silence amid continued arguments.

"This alliance is less than a day old," he said, "and already we're at each other's throats while the real enemy sails closer by the hour."

The sergeant of the Dragonkin contingent sneered. "The *boy* speaks. Perhaps when your voice has settled, we might take your opinion into consideration."

Ripples of laughter came from both sides of the room.

"I . . . I just meant . . ." Pryce fumbled, looking to Kai for support, but his friend could only offer a shrug.

Finnegan's walking stick struck the floor three times. The old man rose, coming to stand beside Pryce.

"The lad's right, even if his delivery needs work," Finnegan said. "Squabbling like gulls over a fish carcass while Corsairs sharpen their blades? Madness."

Mayor Wright seized the opening. "Thank you, Pryce, for attempting to bring us back to order. And thank you, Mr. Finnegan, for your wisdom." She turned to address the room. "Now, regarding the provisions dispute . . ."

Pryce sank back into his chair. Kai leaned over and whispered, "Good try. Maybe next time don't let your voice crack like you're twelve again."

"Next time you can stand up and make a fool of yourself," Pryce said.

Across the table, Seren watched him. When their eyes met, she didn't look away, but neither did she offer any encouragement.

The meeting continued around him, his momentary attempt at authority already forgotten by most in the room.

Tobias stood. "We've prepared an inventory of all available food stores. With proper rationing, we can sustain both populations for three weeks. Beyond that, we'll need additional supplies or successful hunting parties."

The sergeant and Markham eyed each other with lingering hostility, but neither spoke.

"A reasonable compromise," Seren said, breaking the tense silence. "My delegation accepts these terms."

Markham opened his mouth to object, but a stern look from Mayor Wright silenced him.

"Very well," the mayor said. "Let's move on to the next item: joint patrols."

By midafternoon, exhaustion pulled at Pryce's shoulders. When Mayor Wright called for a brief recess, he escaped to a small balcony off the main hall. The fresh air revived him somewhat as he gazed out at Lake Dragontide.

"Not running away, I hope," said Seren's voice behind him.

Pryce turned to find the princess standing in the doorway. Without the formality of the council chamber, she seemed almost vulnerable.

"Just catching my breath. Politics is more exhausting than dragon training."

She moved to stand beside him at the railing. "Alliances are built on more than formal agreements. They require individuals who can bridge differences."

Pryce shifted uncomfortably, unsure how to respond to the intensity in her gaze. "The council will be reconvening soon."

"Of course." Seren stepped back. "We should return."

***

The afternoon session proved no less challenging than the morning's deliberations. As the sun began its descent, tension in the chamber had reached a breaking point. Markham and the Dragonkin sergeant—whose name Pryce had learned was Drakonir—circled each other like territorial predators, each looking for weaknesses in the other's arguments.

The current dispute concerned watch rotations along Crystal Shores' western approach.

"Shorling eyes can't see in darkness like ours can," Drakonir insisted, looming over the map table. "Dragonkin should take all night watches."

"And have your warriors reporting only to your command?" Markham said. "Conveniently forgetting to mention important details? No. Each watch must be mixed—Shorling and Dragonkin together."

"You dare question our honor?" Drakonir said.

"I question your motives," Markham said. "Six months ago, you were invading our village. Now we're supposed to trust you with our security?"

"Without us, there would be no homes left to defend!" Drakonir shouted, rising suddenly. His scales darkened with rage as he seized a ceremonial dagger from his belt and drove it into the ancient table, where it quivered between two territorial maps. Several Shorling councilors instinctively recoiled from the display of Dragonkin temper.

Before Pryce could intervene, Markham lunged forward, grabbing the front of Drakonir's armor. With surprising strength for his age, the councilor yanked the Dragonkin sergeant forward until their faces were inches apart.

"One wrong move," Markham said, "one sign of treachery, and I'll personally ensure you regret it."

Drakonir's hand went to his weapon. Other Dragonkin warriors rose from their seats. The alliance teetered on the edge of dissolution.

"STOP!" Pryce shouted. "Councilor Markham, release him. Now."

For a moment, Pryce thought Markham would refuse. Then, with obvious reluctance, the older man released his grip on Drakonir's armor.

Pryce turned to face both delegations. "Look at ourselves. Fighting over watch schedules while Corsairs prepare to attack. This is exactly what they want—for us to be divided."

He moved to the map, placing his finger on the western approach to Crystal Shores. "Mixed watches," he said firmly. "Two Shorlings, two Dragonkin on each patrol. They report to both commands simultaneously. Any objections?"

Hostility in the room was high, but no one objected.

"Good," Pryce continued. "Now, unless someone has another petty grievance to air, I suggest we focus on what really matters—defending Crystal Shores."

He turned to Seren. "Princess, do the Dragonkin accept these terms?"

After a pause, she inclined her head. "We do."

"Councilor Markham? On behalf of Crystal Shores?"

Markham's mustache twitched, but he nodded stiffly. "Accepted."

"Then this council is adjourned until tomorrow morning," Mayor Wright announced, bringing down her gavel with an air of relief.

As the delegations filed out, the tension in the room slowly dissipated. Kai approached Pryce, eyebrows raised.

"That was unexpected," he said. "Where did all that authority come from?"

"I just couldn't watch them destroy everything we're trying to build."

"Well, it worked. Even Markham looked impressed, in his grumpy, I'd-rather-die-than-admit-it way."

From across the emptying chamber, Pryce caught Seren watching him. She gave him a slight nod before turning to leave with her delegation.

As Pryce gathered his notes, movement caught his eye. Near one of the tall windows. For a brief moment, he glimpsed what looked like a patchwork cloak.

"Did you see that?" he asked Kai.

"See what?" Kai looked up from where he'd been collecting discarded cups.

"By the window. I thought I saw . . ." Pryce crossed to the window, but found nothing. Yet on the sill lay a small, intricately carved wooden token, its surface marked with symbols.

When he picked it up, it felt warm, as if recently held. The token bore intricate spiraling patterns that seemed to shift as he turned it in his fingers. At its center was an unmistakable symbol—a tiny flame surrounded by three interlocking circles.

"What's that?" Kai asked, peering over his shoulder.

"A Quibnocket token," Pryce said. "My mother told me about these."

His mind filled with Ellie's stories—tales of a mischievous creature named Pipwhistle who had helped her during her most desperate hours. "Neither friend nor foe, but something in between," she'd told him once. "The Quibnockets appear when the tides of fate shift, always with a purpose, though rarely a straightforward one."

Ellie had described Pipwhistle in detail: the patchwork cloak that seemed to hold pieces of every traveler's garment, the wiry hair that moved as if in a breeze even on still days, the laughter like tiny bells that gave away his hiding places. She'd shown Pryce the Royal Sapphire—a wedding gift from Pipwhistle himself—and warned him to guard his pockets if he ever encountered the trickster.

"You're joking, right?" Kai looked skeptical. "Those are just stories to frighten children into keeping their hands in their pockets."

"My mother doesn't tell stories to frighten anyone," Pryce said, turning the token over. On the reverse side was carved a single word: Beware.

"Pipwhistle," Pryce whispered, convinced now of the token's origin. "But beware of what?"

"Maybe it means beware of councils full of angry Dragonkin and stubborn Shorlings," Kai said, though his attempt at humor fell flat.

Pryce slipped the token into his pocket. "My mother trusted Pipwhistle, despite his trickster nature. There must be something important he's trying to warn us about."

The wind changed direction suddenly, carrying a scent of rain and something else—something like burnt cinnamon. Then it was gone.

Outside, the sun slipped below the horizon. Somewhere to the west, Corsair ships drew closer.

CHAPTER 6

Kai pocketed his notes from the day's meeting. "I don't know about you, but after that diplomatic nightmare, I could use a drink."

"Water?" Pryce asked with a half-smile.

"I was thinking cloudberry fizz at the Rusty Anchor," Kai said. "Tobias mentioned he'd be there tonight. It might do you good to remember what normal conversation sounds like."

Pryce fingered the Quibnocket token in his pocket, its carved warning—*Beware*—still troubling him. Perhaps an evening among friends was exactly what he needed to clear his head.

"Fine. But just for a little while. Tomorrow's council starts early."

They made their way through Crystal Shores' winding streets as evening settled over the village. Lanterns flickered to life in windows, and the distant sound of waves lapping against the docks provided a soothing counterpoint to the day's heated debates.

The Rusty Anchor's sign creaked in the evening breeze, its painted anchor faded from years of sun. Inside, lanterns cast a warm glow over rough-hewn tables and the bar counter where Brim, the proprietor, polished glasses.

Pryce paused at the threshold, taken aback by the scene before him. The Rusty Anchor was more crowded than he'd ever seen it. Shorling fishermen huddled near the hearth, their voices low. Dragonkin warriors occupied tables near the windows. The two groups maintained a careful distance from each other.

"This doesn't look promising," Pryce said to Kai.

"Look, there's Tobias." Kai nodded toward a corner table where he sat alone, nursing a mug and watching the room.

They weaved through the crowd, nodding awkwardly to familiar faces.

"You look like you've been trampled by Old Man Doyle's goat herd," Tobias said as Pryce collapsed onto the bench beside him.

"Feel like it too." Pryce signaled Lina, the server, for a mug of cloudberry fizz—the non-alcoholic beverage that had become Crystal Shores' specialty. "Negotiating peace is harder than fighting a war."

Tobias leaned forward, his merchant's cap pushed back on his head. "Word is you stood up to Councilor Markham and that Dragonkin sergeant."

"And lived to tell the tale," Kai added. "Our boy's becoming a proper diplomat."

"Diplomat. Peacekeeper. Target." Pryce shrugged. "Take your pick."

Lina arrived with a round of cloudberry fizz. "Careful out there tonight," she whispered, nodding toward a particularly rowdy table of Dragonkin warriors. "They've been drinking since sundown, and not the watered-down stuff."

"Thanks for the warning," Pryce said.

As Lina retreated, a burst of laughter erupted from the Dragonkin table. Drakonir raised his mug high. "To alliance with these . . . fishfolk!" he said, the slight pause before "fishfolk" making it clear a less complimentary term had been his first choice.

"They're not even trying to hide their contempt," Tobias said.

Across the room, Gordan Flintjaw—once Pryce's childhood bully, now civil—slammed his tankard down. "Hear that? They mock us in our own tavern!"

"Easy, Gordan," Pryce called. "It's been a long day for everyone."

"Defending them now, Harper-Green?" Gordan's eyes narrowed. "First you get scales, then you get engaged to one of them. What's next—gills and a tail?"

A ripple of uneasy laughter spread among the Shorling tables. Pryce's hand instinctively rose to the faint scale pattern still visible along his jaw—a permanent reminder of the Dragonkin's attempt to transform him six months earlier.

"Leave him be, Gordan," Tobias said. "Pryce is the reason we have ships protecting our harbor."

"At what cost?" Gordan said. "Trading Crystal Shores' future to our enemies in exchange for a few warships and a princess bride?"

The Dragonkin warrior stood, swaying slightly. "You speak of costs? What of ours, aligning with village-folk who can barely navigate beyond sight of shore?"

"Better close to shore than close to treachery," Gordan shot back.

Pryce dropped his head into his hands. "And here we go."

"Bets on who throws the first punch?" Kai whispered. "My money's on Gordan. He's been itching for a fight since the Dragonkin arrived."

"No one's throwing any punches," Pryce said.

Drakonir staggered toward Gordan's table, his companions trailing behind with predatory grins. "You Shorlings think yourselves so righteous, yet without us, the Corsairs would already be dividing your village among themselves."

"We managed just fine before you scaled invaders appeared," Gordan stood, squaring his shoulders. Though he lacked the warrior's height, his fisherman's build was solid from hauling nets.

Brim moved from behind the bar, dish towel still in hand. "Now, gentlemen, the Rusty Anchor has house rules about brawling. Take your disagreements outside or settle them peacefully."

The warrior turned his eyes toward Brim. "Peace? Is that what you call hiding behind your walls while others fight your battles?"

"No one's hiding," Pryce said, rising from his seat. "And no one's fighting, not here."

"Ah, the dragon-tamer speaks." The warrior's gaze shifted to Pryce, a cruel smile playing across his scaled features. "Tell me, boy, did your courage die with your honor when you agreed to marry our princess? Or were you always this spineless?"

Pryce felt Kai tense beside him, ready to leap to his defense, but he placed a restraining hand on his friend's arm. "I'm just trying to keep the peace. Same as everyone else here."

"Peace." The warrior spat the word like a curse. "Your kind wouldn't recognize true peace if it swam up and bit you. Your father proves that— running off to Port Ravenspur at the first sign of trouble."

A hush fell over the tavern. Even the most intoxicated patrons recognized the dangerous territory the conversation had entered.

"My father," Pryce said, "is meeting with Captain Henley on diplomatic business. You'd do well to mind your words."

"Diplomatic business," the warrior mimicked, his voice rising. "Is that what Shorlings call abandoning their village? No wonder your princess refused to marry you the first time—why bind herself to a family of cowards?"

Gordan stepped forward, fists clenched, but Pryce waved him back. The Quibnocket token burned in his pocket like a hot coal, its warning— *Beware*—suddenly taking on new meaning.

"That's enough," Pryce said. "You're drunk. Go back to your table, and we'll forget this conversation happened."

Another Dragonkin warrior joined his companion. "Listen to the boy, Drakonir. His kind are good at forgetting—they've forgotten how quickly we could reduce this village to cinders, just as they've forgotten whose protection they now depend on."

Pryce's patience frayed further, but he held his temper in check. "We remember everything. Just as we remember who helped defeat your Queen's forces six months ago."

"With a secondhand storm dragon," Drakonir sneered. "A pathetic creature too weak to serve in a proper military squadron."

Pryce's hand tightened around his mug.

"What was its name again?" the darker-scaled warrior asked with mock thoughtfulness. "Stormwing? More like Storm *whelp*. We have messenger birds with more battle prowess."

Something snapped inside Pryce. The insults to his family, his village, even himself—those he could endure. But Stormwing was different. The dragon had saved Crystal Shores, had saved *him*, countless times.

"Take it back," Pryce said, his voice dropping low.

"What's that, Shorling?" Drakonir leaned closer, cupping his ear in exaggerated fashion. "Did the half-scale boy finally find his voice?"

"I said," Pryce repeated, setting down his mug and taking a deliberate step toward the Dragonkin warrior, "take back what you said about Stormwing."

The warrior laughed. "Or what? You'll send your oversized lizard to frighten me? That creature couldn't scare a—"

Pryce's fist connected with Drakonir's jaw before the Dragonkin could finish his sentence. The crack of impact silenced the tavern for one stunned heartbeat.

Drakonir staggered back, eyes wide with shock as he touched his bleeding lip. Then chaos erupted.

Tables overturned as Shorlings and Dragonkin collided in a tangle of limbs and shouted curses. Mugs shattered against walls. A chair flew across the room, splintering against a support beam.

"By the lake's depths, Pryce!" Kai ducked as a tankard sailed over his head. "When you decide to start a fight, you don't mess around!"

"I didn't mean to—" Pryce began, then had to dive sideways as Drakonir lunged for him.

The warrior tackled him into a table, sending cloudberry fizz spraying across three bystanders who immediately joined the fray. Pryce managed to roll free, coming up in a crouch as fishermen and Dragonkin guards grappled around him.

Gordan, surprisingly, appeared at Pryce's side. "Never thought I'd see the day," he said, fending off a Dragonkin with a right hook. "Harper-Green starting a tavern brawl! Your father would be proud!"

"He most certainly would not!" Pryce shouted over the commotion, dodging another wild swing.

Across the room, Brim had taken shelter behind the bar, occasionally rising to spray combatants with water from a pressure pump usually reserved for cleaning mugs. "You're all banned!" he bellowed, though no one paid him any mind.

Tobias slid across a table, boots first, knocking two Dragonkin warriors into each other. "Like fishing crates in a storm!" he called gleefully. "Stack 'em and rack 'em!"

The fighting spread to every corner of the tavern. Lina, the server, abandoned neutrality and was using her serving tray as both shield and weapon. Even Old Man Finnegan had appeared from somewhere, his walking stick becoming a surprisingly versatile combat tool as he tripped Dragonkin warriors.

"Six months ago, I was fighting for my life against these same people," Kai shouted as he ducked beneath a wild swing. "Now I'm brawling with them in a tavern. Progress?"

Pryce couldn't answer. He was too busy trying to avoid Drakonir's increasingly focused attacks. The Dragonkin warrior had singled him out, ignoring easier targets to pursue Pryce through the chaos.

"You dare strike me, Shorling?" Drakonir lunged forward again.

Pryce sidestepped, using a move Stormwing had inadvertently taught him during their early training sessions—a quick twist that used his opponent's momentum against him. Drakonir crashed into the bar, sending glasses and bottles cascading to the floor.

For a moment, Pryce thought he might have ended the confrontation. Then Drakonir rose, shards of glass glittering in his scales like jewels.

"Now you die," he growled, drawing a dagger from his belt.

The sight of actual steel transformed the nature of the brawl. Shorlings scrambled backward, and even other Dragonkin paused in their fighting.

Kai appeared at Pryce's side, spear in hand.

"That's enough!" A commanding voice cut through the noise.

Princess Seren stood in the tavern doorway, her scales darkening with anger as she surveyed the destruction. Behind her, Dragonkin royal guards formed an imposing presence.

"Princess," Drakonir said, immediately sheathing his dagger and dropping to one knee. The other Dragonkin warriors followed suit, suddenly looking considerably more sober.

"Is this how you represent our people?" Seren's voice was quiet but carried throughout the now-silent tavern. "Brawling like common mercenaries? Drawing weapons on allies?"

"Your Highness," Drakonir began, "the Shorling struck first—"

"After considerable provocation, I imagine," Seren cut him off. Her gaze moved to Pryce, who stood amid the wreckage, blood trickling from a split lip. "Is that how it happened, Pryce Harper-Green?"

All eyes turned to him. Pryce could feel the weight of both sides' expectations—the Shorlings wanting him to hold the Dragonkin accountable, the Dragonkin warriors silently warning him against crossing their princess.

"The fault was mine," Pryce said finally. "I lost my temper. Struck the first blow."

A murmur of disbelief rippled through the Shorling onlookers. Even Gordan stared at him with newfound respect.

"Indeed?" Seren raised an eyebrow, her violet eyes studying him intently. "And what provocation could possibly justify such an action from someone tasked with maintaining our alliance?"

Pryce's hand moved instinctively to where his bow would be. "He insulted Stormwing. Called her weak."

"I see," she said. Then, turning to her guards: "Remove these warriors from the tavern. They will be disciplined appropriately."

"But Your Highness—" Drakonir said.

"You insult a rider's dragon, you accept the consequences," Seren said coldly. "Be grateful he used his fist rather than calling Stormwing herself to settle the matter."

As the Dragonkin warriors were escorted out, Brim emerged fully from behind the bar, surveying the devastation with a pained expression. Broken chairs and tables lay scattered across the floor. Splashes of cloudberry fizz stained the walls. The remnants of at least three fish stews dripped from the ceiling.

"I expect full compensation for damages," he told Pryce, his normally jovial face creased with displeasure.

"Of course," Pryce winced, imagining the cost. "I'll see to it personally."

The tavern gradually emptied as Shorlings began the awkward process of returning to their homes, casting backward glances at Pryce that ranged from admiration to confusion to outright disapproval.

Soon only Kai, Tobias, and a few stragglers remained, helping Brim and Lina right overturned furniture and sweep up broken glass.

"Well," Kai said, examining a splinter embedded in his palm, "that was certainly more exciting than council meetings."

"I punched a Dragonkin warrior," Pryce said, the reality of his actions finally sinking in. "I started a tavern brawl. What was I thinking?"

"You were defending Stormwing's honor," Tobias said. "Any dragon rider would have done the same."

"I'm supposed to be maintaining the alliance, not shattering it along with half the tavern's inventory." Pryce groaned, dropping onto a miraculously intact chair. "My parents are going to kill me when they return."

"If it helps," Lina said as she swept past with a broom, "I've never seen Gordan look at you with such respect. You might have actually earned some credibility with the hardliners tonight."

"At the cost of the Dragonkin's trust," Pryce said.

"I wouldn't be so sure about that," Kai said, nodding toward the door.

Princess Seren had returned, this time without her guards. She stood in the doorway, moonlight silhouetting her figure.

"A word, Pryce Harper-Green?" she said, her tone making it clear this was not optional.

Pryce exchanged a quick glance with his friends before joining her outside. The night air was cool, carrying the familiar scents of lake water and fish oil that defined Crystal Shores.

"Your Highness, I—"

"Loyalty is a rare trait," Seren interrupted, her gaze fixed on the harbor. "Especially loyalty that transcends species."

"Stormwing is more than just a mount," Pryce said. "She's . . ."

"Family," Seren finished for him. "Yes, I understand better than you might think."

She turned to face him. "Your actions tonight were foolish, impulsive, and completely inappropriate for someone in your position."

Pryce braced himself for what would surely be a diplomatic catastrophe.

"They were also," Seren continued, "exactly what I would have done had someone insulted my dragon in such a manner."

Pryce blinked in surprise. "You're not angry?"

"Oh, I'm furious," Seren assured him. "This incident damages our carefully constructed alliance, undermines what little trust we've built, and sets a terrible example for both our peoples."

She stepped closer, close enough that Pryce could see the subtle patterns in her scales. "But I respect your loyalty to Stormwing. It . . . complicates my opinion of you."

"I'm sorry for the trouble I've caused.".

"Are you?" Seren asked. "Because watching you defend your dragon with such ferocity, I suspect a part of you found satisfaction in that moment of truth."

Pryce couldn't deny it—landing that punch had felt righteous in a way that hours of diplomatic maneuvering never had.

"Tomorrow will be difficult," Seren warned. "The council will hear of this, and there will be consequences." She turned to leave, then paused. "But tonight . . . tonight you reminded me that there is more to you than politics and compromise, Pryce Harper-Green. You reminded me why I once thought you might be worthy of respect."

With that, she departed, leaving Pryce alone beneath the stars, wondering if he'd just destroyed the alliance—or somehow strengthened it.

From the tavern behind him came the sound of Kai's voice raised in an improvised shanty about "the night Pryce Harper-Green found his fist." Despite everything, Pryce found himself smiling.

Sometimes, it seemed, peace required a well-placed punch.

CHAPTER 7

Pryce expected to wake sore, and did. He expected to wake exhausted, and did. He expected to wake as the least popular dragon-trainer in the village, and most definitely did. What he didn't expect was to wake smiling, and yet here he was, a grin tugging at his swollen lip.

He slipped into the council chamber before sunrise, hoping the early hour would grant him a few moments of solitude before facing the village's judgment. His knuckles throbbed, the skin split and scabbed from connecting with Drakonir's jaw the previous night.

He winced as he lowered himself into a chair, discovering fresh bruises he hadn't noticed. How quickly things had changed—yesterday, he'd been the reluctant diplomat. Today? The hothead who'd thrown the first punch.

"You look like you've been trampled by a herd of lake oxen," came Councilor Markham's voice from the doorway. For once, the perpetually disgruntled man seemed almost amused rather than disapproving. "Word travels fast in a fishing village. Half the harbor's talking about how you laid out that Dragonkin warrior."

"It wasn't my finest moment."

"Perhaps not," Markham said, settling into a chair with a grunt. "But there are worse things than showing those scaled intruders we've got limits to our patience." He leaned forward conspiratorially. "Between us, boy, a few think you've finally grown a backbone."

Pryce stared at his hands. The irony wasn't lost on him—he'd spent yesterday struggling to be heard in council, and now he'd gained respect through violence. What kind of leader did that make him?

More councilors filed in, each greeting him differently than before. Some nodded with newfound respect. Others kept their distance, as if his recklessness might be contagious. Tobias gave him a subtle thumbs-up behind Westley's back. Finnegan simply tapped his walking stick against the floor twice as he passed—an old signal of approval among fishermen.

Mayor Wright arrived last, her spectacles perched on her nose, her expression neutral as she caught Pryce's eye.

"Before we begin," she said once everyone had settled, "I'd like to address last night's . . . incident . . . at the Rusty Anchor."

The room fell silent, all eyes turning to Pryce.

"While I understand emotions are running high, and provocations were made," Mayor Wright continued, "we cannot afford such displays at this critical juncture. That said, what's done is done. Today we focus on maintaining our alliance and preparing for the Corsair threat."

She spread maps across the table—harbor defense diagrams, patrol routes, supply inventories—and launched into details of Crystal Shores' preparations.

"Joint patrols have reported no sign of Corsair ships since yesterday," she was saying, "but our eastern lookouts have spotted—"

The council chamber doors swung open with deliberate force.

In the doorway stood a Dragonkin male Pryce had hoped never to see again. Scarlet scales gleamed at his temples, extending down his neck like fresh blood. His tall, athletic frame was now adorned with the elaborate armor of a Dragonkin battlemaster— clearly a recent promotion. His precise movements as he entered the chamber reminded everyone present of his extensive warrior training.

Thane Zharan had arrived.

Conversations died. Backs straightened. Hands that had been relaxed now gripped chair edges or rested near concealed weapons.

"Battlemaster Thane," Mayor Wright said. "We weren't informed you would be joining us."

Speaking with an air of noble superiority, Thane said, "Queen Nymeria felt a military presence would benefit these proceedings, particularly given recent . . . lapses in discipline."

His gaze fixed on Pryce.

"I see our famous dragon-tamer bears the marks of his tavern heroics," Thane continued, with his cultured voice. "How impressive that Crystal Shores' leadership resolves diplomatic challenges with their fists. Perhaps next council meeting should be held in the Rusty Anchor? I hear the ambiance is particularly conducive to thoughtful negotiation."

Pryce's face burned. "Battlemaster Thane. Your concern for our diplomatic protocols is noted."

"Is it?" Thane moved further into the room, forcing others to shift their chairs to accommodate his presence. "Just as your concern for our alliance was so clearly demonstrated when you assaulted Sergeant Drakonir? A decorated warrior with twenty years of service?"

"A decorated warrior who insulted a dragon that saved this village," Finnegan said, his walking stick striking the floor sharply.

Thane's attention shifted to the old man. "Ah, the village elder speaks. Tell me, does Crystal Shores typically allow its youngsters to determine foreign policy through tavern brawls? Or is this a special privilege reserved for those with . . . unusual heritage?" He motioned toward the scales still visible along Pryce's jawline.

"That's enough," Mayor Wright said. "Battlemaster Thane, if you've come to participate constructively in our council, you're welcome to stay. If you're here merely to provoke, perhaps your talents would be better utilized elsewhere."

"My talents, Mayor Wright, include recognizing leadership—or its absence." Thane selected a chair directly across from Pryce. "I wonder what Queen Nymeria will think when she learns her daughter's betrothed resolves conflicts with his fists instead of his mind."

Pryce's stomach twisted. "Princess Seren is already aware of what happened."

"Oh? And did she express her profound admiration for your diplomatic skills?" Thane's voice carried just enough to ensure everyone in the chamber could hear. "Or perhaps she's reconsidering the wisdom of aligning with a village whose representative cannot control impulses?"

"Battlemaster," Mayor Wright interrupted firmly, "we have pressing matters regarding coastal defense to discuss. Your military expertise would be valuable, should you choose to contribute it."

With obvious reluctance, Thane allowed the conversation to shift back to defense preparations. Throughout the meeting, however, he inserted subtle barbs whenever Pryce spoke, questioning his suggestions with raised eyebrows or faint smirks that undermined without direct confrontation.

By the time the council adjourned two hours later, Pryce felt as if he'd been through another physical fight—though this one had left no visible bruises, only the lingering ache of humiliation.

As the chamber emptied, Kai approached. "That scale-faced snake," he said, glancing toward Thane's retreating back. "He didn't come here to help with defense planning. He came to undermine you specifically."

Pryce sighed, gathering his notes. "I noticed."

"It's not just politics," Kai said, leaning closer. "The way he looked at you—that was personal. Do you know why?"

"Thane's father was disgraced years ago—something involving my parents. The details always seemed unimportant until now."

Kai frowned. "He's got it out for you specifically."

"Doesn't matter. We need the Dragonkin alliance to survive the Corsair threat. If that means enduring Thane's provocations, so be it."

"And if his 'provocations' go beyond words? What then?"

Pryce looked toward the door where Thane had disappeared. "Then we deal with that when it happens. For now, we focus on protecting Crystal Shores."

But as they left the chamber, Pryce couldn't shake the feeling that Thane Zharan represented a threat as dangerous as any Corsair ship.

***

The training grounds sprawled across a flat stretch of packed dirt near the eastern harbor, where Shorling guards had drilled for generations. Today, they moved through formations with extra vigor, each soldier keenly aware of the Dragonkin observers watching from the shade of a nearby storage shed. Pryce followed Mayor Wright across the grounds. The fresh air should have been a relief after the stifling chamber, but knowing Thane Zharan stood among those observers transformed even this open space into another battlefield.

"They're putting on quite a show today," Kai said, falling into step beside Pryce. "Ever notice how everyone stands a little straighter when being watched by giants with scales?"

A dozen Shorling guards moved through combat drills under Westley's direction, armed primarily with spears and short swords. Although Westley was the harbormaster by title, he had honed Oceanrider skills over the years, often stepping in to fill the gap while the main Oceanrider navy was away. Behind them stood a hastily constructed obstacle course that followed the contours of the harbor's edge, offering both physical challenges and strategic cover points.

"The council meeting could have gone worse," Pryce said, keeping his voice low as they approached the training area.

"Yes, Thane could have actually stabbed you instead of just fantasizing about it," Kai said. "I counted at least three times when his hand moved to his dagger."

Pryce was about to respond when Thane stepped from the observers' shade. The Dragonkin battlemaster approached the training guards with the confident stride of someone accustomed to commanding attention. Unlike the other Dragonkin who maintained a distance, Thane walked directly into the training area.

"Harbormaster Westley," Thane called. "Your guards show commendable basic form, but perhaps I might suggest an adjustment to better prepare them for actual combat?"

Westley hesitated, clearly uncomfortable with the intrusion but unwilling to risk offending a high-ranking Dragonkin during such delicate diplomatic times.

"We welcome any tactical insight, Battlemaster," Mayor Wright answered before Westley could respond. Her tone made it clear this was a political necessity.

Thane smiled, revealing teeth just pointed enough to remind everyone of his predatory heritage. "The Corsairs won't attack in neat formations," he said, addressing the guards directly now. "They swarm from multiple angles, using terrain to their advantage."

He gestured toward the obstacle course. "Your current approach has your men running this course one at a time. In real combat, you must move as coordinated units while maintaining individual awareness."

It sounded reasonable, even helpful. Pryce watched, suspicious but unable to fault the tactical logic.

"Perhaps," Thane continued, "a demonstration? Your four strongest guards could attempt the course together, using the advanced flanking technique we Dragonkin employ against superior numbers."

The old senior oceanriders exchanged glances. Four stepped forward, including Corrin, the seasoned elder and broad-shouldered leader of Crystal Shores' modest defense crew.

Thane positioned the men himself, placing them in a diamond formation and explaining how each should move in relation to the others. He seemed genuinely engaged in the instruction, pointing out details and correcting stances with professional precision.

"Notice how Battlemaster Thane has them holding their shields," Kai whispered. "That's not a standard position for negotiating narrow walkways."

Pryce frowned, observing more closely. Indeed, Thane had adjusted their shield grips to a position that would partially obscure their peripheral vision. Subtle, but potentially significant.

"Begin at Harbormaster Westley's signal," Thane said, stepping back with a respectful bow. "Remember, maintain formation even when the terrain challenges you."

Westley raised his arm, then dropped it sharply. The four guards moved onto the course, maintaining the diamond formation Thane had demonstrated. They navigated the first obstacles with reasonable coordination—climbing over a low wall, ducking under a net of ropes.

"They're doing well," Mayor Wright said, seeming genuinely pleased by the cooperation.

Kai pointed to four parallel wooden planks that spanned a particularly muddy section of ground. Recent rains had transformed what would normally be a simple dirt patch into a deep mud pit.

The guards reached the beams, still maintaining formation as Thane had instructed. Corrin, at the front position, stepped onto his beam first. The others followed on their respective planks.

What happened next occurred so quickly that Pryce almost missed the crucial detail. Thane made a sharp gesture—a signal that could easily be interpreted as encouragement. The rear guard, responding instinctively to what appeared to be a command from an authority figure, adjusted his position precisely as his beam crossed over the deepest section of mud.

The guard's weight shifted. His shield, held in the awkward position Thane had insisted upon, prevented him from seeing that his beam had a subtle curve.

The wood cracked beneath him. He plunged downward with a startled shout, his momentum and the formation Thane had demanded pulling the others off balance. Within seconds, all four guards tumbled into the mud pit, their heavy practice armor dragging them deeper into the unexpectedly thick mire.

Gasps and shouts erupted from the spectators. Pryce rushed forward, suddenly realizing this was no simple training mishap. The pit wasn't just mud—it was a mixture of harbor clay and silt that behaved like quicksand when disturbed.

Corrin struggled to keep his head above the surface, his armor weighing him down. The other guards flailed, each movement only embedding them deeper.

"Rope!" Pryce shouted, wading in at the edge. "They'll sink if they keep struggling!"

Kai had already grabbed coils of practice rope from a nearby rack. He tossed one end to Pryce, who caught it and extended it toward Corrin.

"Grab this," Pryce called. "And stop moving! The more you fight it, the faster you sink."

Thane stood at the edge. "What unfortunate timing. These spring muds can be treacherous."

Working quickly, Pryce and Kai managed to extract the guards one by one. Each emerged covered in foul-smelling muck, gasping and humiliated. The last guard—the youngest—required both Pryce and Kai pulling together to free him from the sucking mud.

"Such poor discipline," Thane commented to the watching Dragonkin observers. "In our training, warriors learn to recognize unstable terrain before charging across it."

Corrin, usually stoic, flushed with humiliation beneath his mask of mud. The other guards looked equally mortified—elite defenders reduced to dripping, stinking spectacles before foreign dignitaries.

"Are you all right?" Pryce asked, helping Corrin remove his mud-clogged helmet.

"Nothing injured except pride," Corrin said, embarresed. "Shouldn't have taken advice from a Dragonkin. My fault."

Pryce's eyes narrowed as he examined the beam closely. A subtle shift in its alignment caught his attention. "This beam was tampered with. Did you notice that?"

Corrin frowned. "What? No, I was focused on maintaining that blasted formation he insisted on."

Pryce needed to examine it closely before making accusations, but he was certain the break hadn't been natural.

Kai approached, having helped the younger guard. "We need to tell Mayor Wright what happened. That was deliberate. Thane set them up to fail."

"We need proof first." Pryce watched as Thane conversed with the mayor, gesturing toward the mud pit with what appeared to be genuine regret. "Without it, we'll just sound like we're trying to shift blame."

"Those guards could have drowned in that mud," Kai said. "That wasn't just humiliation—it was attempted murder disguised as a training accident."

"I know. But Thane's too smart to leave obvious evidence. We need to be careful how we handle this."

As if sensing their discussion, Thane glanced in their direction, a faint smile playing at the corners of his mouth. His eyes met Pryce's across the distance, and in that moment, Pryce knew with absolute certainty—this had only been the opening move in a much more dangerous game.

***

Crystal Shores' village square transformed at dusk. Lanterns hung from ropes stretched between buildings, casting pools of warm light over the gathering crowd. On any normal evening, the atmosphere would have been relaxed—fishermen swapping tales, children chasing each other through the maze of adult legs, traders displaying wares from distant ports. Tonight, however, Pryce caught fragments of his own name, of "training disaster," of "Dragonkin embarrassment."

"They're saying the guards nearly drowned in that mud because you approved some reckless training method," Kai said, appearing at his side with two steaming mugs of cloudberry fizz. He offered one to Pryce. "Apparently, you're now personally responsible for 'undermining Crystal Shores' defenses at a critical time.'"

Pryce accepted the mug but didn't drink. "How did 'Thane's suggested changes that resulted in an accident' become 'Pryce personally endangered guards'?"

"The same way fish stories gain an extra foot with each telling," Kai said. "Except Thane's the fisherman this time, and he's very good at what he does."

Across the square, Thane stood surrounded by a group of villagers, including some of Crystal Shores' most influential merchants. Even from a distance, Pryce could see the Dragonkin battlemaster's charm at work. He laughed at appropriate moments, leaned in with interest when others spoke, and gestured with elegant precision that drew all eyes to his hands—hands that earlier had deliberately positioned guards for what could have been their deaths.

"He's not even bothering to hide his satisfaction," Pryce said.

"Why would he?" Kai replied. "From where they're standing, he tried to help improve our defenses but was undermined by incompetent leadership."

Nearby, Pryce overheard a fisherman speaking in the exaggerated whisper of someone who hopes to be overheard: "First that tavern brawl, now this training disaster. Boy's in over his head. His father would never have allowed such embarrassment."

His companion nodded. "Bad enough we're relying on Dragonkin ships. Worse when our own representative can't maintain basic dignity."

The words stung more than Pryce wanted to admit. He'd spent his life in Crystal Shores, fished with these same men, celebrated village festivals alongside their families. Now they spoke of him as if he were a stranger—or worse, a disappointment.

Thane caught Pryce watching and offered a small, knowing smile before turning back to his audience. He spoke, and though Pryce couldn't hear the words, the effect was immediate—heads turned in Pryce's direction, expressions ranging from disappointment to outright suspicion.

"I should say something," Pryce said, taking a step forward.

Kai placed a restraining hand on his arm. "And confirm whatever narrative Thane just planted? Better to let it cool first."

"While he continues poisoning the village against me?"

"While you gather proof," Kai insisted. "Otherwise, it's just your word against his, and right now—"

"Right now, his word carries more weight," Pryce finished.

A subtle shift in the crowd signaled Princess Seren's arrival. Unlike the previous day's formal procession, tonight she moved through the village square with only two guards. She wore a simpler dress than her usual royal attire, though still finer than anything seen in Crystal Shores.

Pryce braced himself as her path brought her steadily in his direction. Their eyes met across the square, and he read something in her expression that might have been concern, or perhaps simply political calculation.

"Pryce Harper-Green," she said when she reached him, her voice pitched to carry no further than their immediate circle. "I was hoping for a word."

"Of course."

Kai stepped away, giving them space while remaining close enough to intervene if needed. Seren guided Pryce toward a quieter corner of the square, beneath the spreading branches of an ancient oak.

"I've heard troubling reports of today's training exercise," she said once they were relatively isolated. "Four guards nearly lost in harbor mud seems an unusual training outcome."

"It wasn't an accident," Pryce said, keeping his voice low. "The balance beam was tampered with."

"That's a serious accusation."

"It's not an accusation yet. Just an observation."

"And who do you believe might have tampered with training equipment?"

Pryce hesitated. "Thane positioned the guards himself. He insisted on a shield positioning that limited peripheral vision. He signaled for movement at precisely the moment the compromised beam would be under maximum stress."

"You're suggesting a Dragonkin battlemaster deliberately endangered allied forces during peacetime training. Do you understand the diplomatic implications of such a claim?"

"I understand them perfectly," Pryce said. "Which is why I haven't made the claim publicly. But you asked for my assessment, Princess."

Seren studied him. "And what proof do you have that the beam was tampered with, rather than simply giving way under unfortunate circumstances?"

"The cut was too clean. It wasn't weathering or natural weakness."

"Did you examine this beam personally after the incident?"

Pryce's frustration mounted. "By the time the guards were safely extracted, the beam had been cleared away. Convenient, wouldn't you say?"

"What I would say," Seren replied carefully, "is that accusations without evidence serve no one's interests during such delicate times."

"So I should ignore what I saw? Pretend everything is fine while Thane systematically undermines both me and this alliance?"

"What I'm saying is that Thane has served the Dragonkin royal court for years with distinction. His loyalty is unquestioned."

"To the Dragonkin, perhaps. But there's history between his family and mine that you may not be aware of."

For the first time, Seren appeared genuinely surprised. "What history?"

"I don't know the details. My mother mentioned once that Thane's father was disgraced years ago in some incident involving my parents. Whatever happened, Thane blames my family."

Seren glanced across the square to where Thane still held court. "That's concerning. But still insufficient proof of sabotage."

"I know what I saw."

"And I know what the diplomatic consequences would be if you made such accusations without irrefutable evidence." Seren's voice softened. "Be careful, Pryce Harper-Green. Battlemaster Thane is not someone to challenge lightly."

She turned to leave, then paused. "If you truly believe sabotage occurred, find proof. Real proof that could withstand scrutiny from both our peoples."

With that, she left Pryce alone beneath the oak.

He leaned against the trunk, exhausted. How quickly things had unraveled—from respected dragon trainer to village joke in less than two days.

In the square, villagers continued to cast glances his way, their expressions ranging from pity to condemnation. Thane had calculated perfectly— using Crystal Shores' own pride against it. The very qualities Shorlings valued most—competence, dignity, strength—were precisely what he'd undermined in Pryce's public image.

His parents would have known how to handle this. His father would have confronted Thane directly, evidence or not. His mother would have found some diplomatic solution that preserved both the alliance and his reputation.

But his parents weren't here. And Pryce was beginning to suspect that wasn't a coincidence either.

The timing of their summons to Port Ravenspur, Thane's unexpected arrival, the training "accident"—it all felt orchestrated, like pieces moving on one of Old Man Finnegan's strategy boards. But to what end? Did Thane simply want personal revenge? Or was there something larger at stake?

Pryce watched as Thane effortlessly charmed another group of villagers. Whatever the battlemaster's ultimate goal, one thing was becoming increasingly clear—Pryce was running out of time to counter it.

***

Kai had spent eighteen years learning to disappear in Crystal Shores. As the blacksmith's son, he possessed the paradoxical gift of being simultaneously recognized by everyone and noticed by no one. People saw the smith's boy, not Kai himself—which made him perfect for following a Dragonkin battlemaster through winding village streets without arousing suspicion. He'd borrowed his father's leather apron, slung a smith's hammer at his belt, and drifted from one group of villagers to another, always keeping Thane in sight while appearing to be merely delivering messages or collecting payments for his father's work.

Thane paused to speak with a group of fishermen unloading their day's catch. Kai lingered near a stack of empty crates, pretending to examine a loose nail while straining to hear the conversation.

". . . training wouldn't have ended so disastrously if proper protocol had been followed," Thane was saying. "I've commanded warriors without such amateur mishaps."

The fishermen nodded. One—the father of the youngest guard who'd been trapped in the mud— spat onto the dock. "Boy's barely dry behind the ears. His father could handle matters, but him? Out of his depth."

Thane's response was too quiet to hear, but the resulting laughter had an ugly edge. Kai waited until Thane moved on before slipping away himself, careful to maintain distance.

Kai observed a pattern. Thane never explicitly criticized Pryce. Instead, he asked leading questions—"How long has young Harper-Green been acting in council matters?"—or offered sympathetic comments—"Such responsibilities for one so young, especially after yesterday's unfortunate tavern incident."

Each interaction left villagers nodding in agreement, their doubts about Pryce's capabilities subtly reinforced without Thane appearing to have said anything directly negative.

Most unsettling was Thane's encounter with Councilor Markham outside the harbormaster's office. Their exchange had been short yet fiery, with Markham nodding at Thane's words. Despite

Markham's known aversion to the dragonkin, he had swiftly made his way toward the council hall with an uncharacteristic sense of urgency.

Kai followed Thane to the Rusty Anchor. Rather than enter, he circled around to the fishers' alley that ran behind the tavern, slipping through a narrow passage that brought him to Pryce's waiting spot.

"He's inside now," Kai said, finding Pryce concealed in the shadow of a rain barrel. "Buying drinks for half the harbor patrol from the looks of it."

"What did you learn?"

"He's systematic," Kai said, settling beside his friend. "Never accuses you directly, just plants seeds. 'Such a burden for young shoulders.' 'Inexperience can be costly in dangerous times.' Always with that concerned expression, like he's genuinely worried about Crystal Shores."

"Who's he targeting specifically?"

"Fishermen with sons in the guard. Council members. Anyone connected to harbor defense." Kai paused. "And he had a private meeting with Councilor Markham that looked . . . significant."

"Markham never liked my father. He'd be an easy ally for Thane."

"That's not all," Kai continued. "Thane spent nearly an hour with the surviving sailors from Shelter Cove. Asked detailed questions about the

Corsair attack patterns, ship configurations, weapons."

"That could be legitimate military intelligence gathering," Pryce said.

"Maybe. But he was particularly interested in their descriptions of the Corsair commander—kept asking if they'd seen a specific captain with distinctive scars."

"You think he knows this captain personally?"

Kai shrugged. "Can't say. But he seemed unusually focused on finding him."

Pryce's fingers unconsciously traced the faint scale pattern along his jawline—a habit he'd developed when deep in thought.

"There's something else," Kai said, his voice dropping lower. "I overheard him speaking with his guards in Dragonkin. My father taught me a few words for trade purposes." He frowned. "I couldn't understand most of it, but I caught 'princess' and 'betrothal' several times. And your name."

"Could be discussing our engagement," Pryce said. "It's no secret."

"The way they laughed afterward didn't sound like wedding planning. And there was another word I recognized—'kresshar.' My father says it means 'to remove an obstacle.'"

Their eyes met in the dim light.

"I need proof," Pryce said finally. "Not just suspicions or overheard fragments. Something concrete that even Princess Seren couldn't dismiss."

"And how do you propose to get that? Thane's too careful to leave evidence lying around."

"Everyone makes mistakes eventually. Especially when they think they're winning."

Kai studied his friend's face. "You've got that look—the same one you had right before suggesting we rescue that storm dragon everyone else thought was about to eat the village."

"That worked out well enough," Pryce said with a hint of his old smile.

"Near-death experiences aside, yes," Kai sighed. "What's the plan?"

"First, we need to secure what's left of that training beam—if it hasn't already been destroyed. Second, we watch Thane's movements more carefully. He'll need to report to someone about his progress."

"You think he's working with others?"

"A battlemaster doesn't sabotage training exercises for personal amusement," Pryce said. "There's a larger game here, and we need to understand it before making any accusations."

Kai nodded slowly. "I'll check the storage shed where they keep damaged training equipment. If the beam's there, I can get it to your workshop without drawing attention."

"Good," Pryce said. "Meanwhile, I need to speak with Corrin and the other guards who fell into that pit. They might have noticed something we missed."

They parted ways in the dusk, Kai headed toward the training grounds while Pryce made his way to the harbor.

From his position on the harbor wall, Pryce could see the Rusty Anchor's open door, light and laughter spilling onto the street. Thane stood framed in that doorway. Crystal Shores villagers—fishermen, merchants, guards—clustered nearby, hanging on his every word.

Pryce felt something settling inside him—a clarity of purpose that had been missing since the tavern brawl. Thane wanted to destroy him, to undermine the alliance, perhaps even to threaten Crystal Shores itself. The battlemaster had advantages experience and status on his side.

But Pryce had something Thane didn't: the truth. And he would find a way to make that truth known, whatever the cost.

As darkness claimed the harbor and Thane's laughter carried across the water, Pryce turned away. The game had changed. No longer would he simply react to Thane's manipulations—now he would hunt for proof, build his case, and when the moment came, he would be ready.

Behind him, Lake Dragontide stretched vast and dark, hiding Corsair ships somewhere beyond the horizon. But the more immediate threat stood in plain sight, wrapped in Dragonkin scales and diplomatic smiles, working to divide Crystal Shores from within before any enemy ships could reach its shores.

CHAPTER 8

Dawn hadn't yet broken over Crystal Shores when Pryce slipped from his bed in his parents' house. He had slept poorly, his mind replaying Thane's phoney smiles and the villagers' shifting loyalties like a fisherman's net full of squirming eels. After dressing quietly, his joints still aching from the tavern brawl, he went to check on his younger sister, Faye. Seeing her bedroom empty, he knew she must already be at her aviary, tending to her messenger birds.

The aviary stood at the eastern edge of the village, a domed structure of wood and wire mesh that housed Faye's prized Tidewing gulls. Light glowed from within. Pryce pushed open the door to find his younger sister moving among her feathered charges, her red curls tied back in a braid.

"You're up early," Faye said without turning. She offered a strip of dried fish to a gray-and-white gull perched on her wrist. The bird accepted it before allowing Faye to attach a tiny message capsule to its leg.

"Couldn't sleep," Pryce said. He approached slowly, careful not to startle the birds. "Sending warnings?"

"Updates to the coastal villages." Faye gently stroked the gull's head with one finger before carrying it to a perch near an open window. "Three gulls north, two south. Skye will take one to Jorr on Emberfall."

Pryce suddenly recognized the bird Faye had been holding. "Skye!" A grin spread across his face. The bird tilted her head and let out a soft squawk as if acknowledging him. "I missed you, girl," Pryce said warmly, extending an arm for Skye to hop onto. As she settled onto his shoulder with a gentle flutter of wings, he chuckled. "I hope you've been keeping Ash on his toes."

Faye adjusted the strap of her satchel and smiled at the reunion. "She's been quite the messenger. Always swooping in with perfect timing. She even managed to dodge that storm last week like it was just another breeze." Faye reached out to gently stroke Skye's back, earning another approving squawk from the bird.

"Any news from Port Ravenspur? From mom and dad?"

Faye shook her head. "Tell me the truth. How bad is it?"

Pryce leaned against a feeding table as Skye flew to a windowsill. "Thane's turning the village against me. He orchestrated that training accident yesterday. Nearly killed four guards."

"I heard." Faye's fingers moved deftly, preparing another message capsule. "Gordan's cousin was telling everyone at the well that you approved some dangerous Dragonkin training method."

"That's not what—"

"I know." She touched his arm briefly. "But people believe what they want to believe. Especially when the person telling them wears battlemaster insignia and speaks with absolute confidence."

"I need proof of what he's doing. Without it, I'm just the reckless boy who started a tavern brawl and can't control the council."

Faye studied him, seeming older than her fifteen years. "You need space to think. Somewhere away from everyone watching you."

"Emberfall," Pryce said. "I need to check on Jorr anyway, see how the sanctuary's coming along."

"Take Kai. Don't go alone. Not with Thane watching your every move."

Pryce nodded. Besides, Kai had been restless since their investigation began, eager for action rather than observation.

An hour later, Stormwing soared into the sky above Crystal Shores. Skye followed closely. Kai sat behind Pryce on Stormwing's back, gripping the saddle strap with one hand while balancing his spear across his knees with the other.

"Next time we plan a strategic retreat, could we maybe consider a nice, ground-based option?" Kai shouted over the wind. "A stroll along the beach perhaps? Or maybe a gentle wagon ride?"

Pryce smiled. Below them, Crystal Shores shrank to a cluster of tiny buildings, its politics and tensions reduced to insignificance by distance and altitude.

Stormwing banked westward, her broad wings catching the updraughts that carried them toward the distant silhouette of Island of Emberfall. Unlike Crystal Shores' gentle shores, Emberfall rose jagged from the water, volcanic rock thrusting skyward from the lake's surface.

They descended in wide spirals, Stormwing's shadow racing them across the black sand beaches. As they neared the island's surface, warm air enveloped them—the natural heat of the volcanic vents that dotted Emberfall's slopes.

"Smells like rotten eggs," Kai said as they touched down. "Ah, the sweet aroma of vacation."

"You're not used to the smell yet?" Pryce asked, dismounting and stretching his cramped legs. "The hot springs are full of it."

Already, he could feel tension releasing from his shoulders. Stormwing seemed to feel it too, stretching her neck toward the sky and releasing a satisfied rumble before heading toward a larger paddock where she could rest. As Pryce watched her go, he felt a soft nudge against his leg. Glancing down, he saw Ash weaving through his feet with an air of nonchalance only a cat could muster.

They found Jorr near the eastern paddocks, where he worked to repair a feeding trough. The young Dragonkin looked up at their approach.

"Didn't expect visitors today," he said, setting down his tools. "Especially not the acting councilor of Crystal Shores."

"Don't remind me. I'm just Pryce today. No titles, no politics."

Jorr noticed Pryce's exhausted posture and the bruise along his jaw. "Things are difficult in the village." It wasn't a question.

"You could say that," Kai said, leaning on his spear. "If by 'difficult' you mean 'teetering on the edge of diplomatic disaster while a Dragonkin battlemaster systematically undermines our friend here.'"

Jorr gestured for them to follow him toward a natural spring that bubbled near the paddock's edge.

"Dragons don't concern themselves with politics," he said as they walked. "They judge by actions, not words. By loyalty, not appearance." He dipped a ladle into the spring water, offering it to Pryce. "There's peace in that simplicity."

The water tasted of minerals, sharp and clean.

"How are the repairs coming?" Pryce asked, looking around at the half-rebuilt paddocks and shelter areas. "The sanctuary's really taking shape."

"Slowly but steadily," Jorr said. "The dragonets are adapting well. Emberstriker is becoming quite the personality."

"Still stealing bits of clothing?" Kai asked, recalling the dragonet's mischievous habits.

"Only from visitors she likes," Jorr said with a smile. "Come, I'll show you the new nesting area I've prepared for—"

He stopped abruptly, focus shifting to something beyond Pryce's shoulder.

"What is it?" Pryce turned to follow his gaze.

"The south paddock gate," Jorr said, already moving toward it with long strides. "Something's wrong."

They hurried after him. The gate hung slightly askew, one side lower than it should have been. Jorr knelt beside the main support post, examining the rope that secured the crossbeam.

"This splice," he said. "I completed it yesterday. Ten perfect cross-weaves with a double-back pattern."

Pryce crouched beside him, examining the damage. The rope had been cut nearly through in three places, the fresh cuts poorly disguised with mud to look like natural wear.

"Someone did this deliberately," Pryce said. "They wanted it to look like normal deterioration."

"But they didn't know how to properly mimic wear patterns," Jorr added. "A rope doesn't wear from the inside out."

"So much for your peaceful sanctuary. Looks like Thane's reach extends beyond Crystal Shores," Kai said.

Pryce rose slowly, his gaze sweeping across the sanctuary. Suddenly, Emberfall Island didn't feel so separate from Crystal Shores' troubles after all.

"This is expert work," Jorr said, examining the cuts more closely.

"And recent," Pryce added, noticing the fresh splinters where the rope had begun to separate under tension. "Very recent."

Someone had been to Emberfall recently with the deliberate intent to cause harm.

"Let's check the other paddocks," Pryce said. "All of them."

They fanned out across the sanctuary, each taking a section of the dragon refuge. Pryce moved methodically from paddock to paddock, checking each rope junction, each wooden support. It wasn't random vandalism he sought, but the calculated damage of someone who knew exactly what they were doing—and wanted their work discovered too late to prevent harm.

"Here!" Pryce called, examining the eastern paddock gate. Like the first, its support rope had been sliced through beneath a carefully applied layer of mud. The cut was positioned precisely where tension would eventually snap the remaining fibers. "Same technique. They wanted these to fail gradually, not all at once."

"Three more like this. The saboteur knew dragon handling equipment. These cuts are at load-bearing points only handlers would recognize," Jorr said.

Kai called from the nearby storage shed. "You might want to see this."

They found him standing amid sacks of dragon feed, a mixture of dried fish and specialized grains Jorr had developed for the sanctuary's residents. One sack lay open at Kai's feet, its contents scattered across the wooden floor.

"Something's wrong with the feed," Kai said, keeping his distance from the pile. "It smells . . . off."

Jorr knelt beside the spilled feed, reaching for a handful before stopping abruptly. He sniffed carefully, then recoiled. "Don't touch it."

Pryce noticed dark specks mixed throughout the grain. "What is that?"

"Ironfern seeds," Jorr said. "Crushed and mixed in. They cause severe digestive distress in dragons—particularly younger ones."

"Fatal?" Pryce asked.

"It can be, but usually it's extremely painful. It would take days of agony before recovery." Jorr said. "This wasn't meant just to hurt the dragons. It was meant to make them suffer."

Kai wiped his hands on his trousers, though he hadn't touched the tainted feed. "When I agreed to this little excursion, poison testing wasn't on my list of vacation activities."

"We need to check everything," Pryce said, striding toward the door. "Bedding, medical supplies, the whole lot. With Jorr being the only one on the island, aside from the dragons, sabotaging would be a breeze. Plus, make sure Ash stays clear of the feed, and keep an eye on Skye too."

They worked with urgency, discovering subtle sabotage throughout the sanctuary. Training harnesses with weakened stitching. Medicinal herbs replaced with similar-looking but ineffective substitutes. Each instance showed expert knowledge of dragon care—and deliberate malice.

"The water cistern," Jorr said suddenly, his head snapping up. "We need to check the main water supply."

The cistern sat at the sanctuary's heart, a stone-lined basin that collected rainwater for the dragons. A complex system of bamboo pipes directed the water to various pens and bathing areas. Jorr climbed the short ladder to peer inside.

"Hand me that ladle," he said, gesturing to a long-handled dipper hanging nearby.

Pryce climbed up beside him, watching as Jorr collected a sample from the cistern. The water that should have been clear held a strange, almost oily sheen. At the bottom of the ladle, fine white sediment slowly settled.

Jorr sniffed it, then jerked his head back. "Someone's poisoned the water."

"With what?" Pryce asked.

"Limeroot extract, if I'm not mistaken. It causes disorientation, weakness, and eventually paralysis in dragons." Jorr poured the sample. "It dissolves slowly, releasing toxins over time. The dragons might have been drinking it for days already."

Kai gagged at the smell when Jorr showed him the remaining drops in the ladle. "Smells like my father's boots after a week in the smithy," he said. "Remind me not to complain about Crystal Shores' well water again."

"We need to empty the entire cistern. Get fresh water from the higher springs," Pryce said.

"And check the dragons," Jorr added. "Immediately. If any have been drinking this . . ."

A weak hiss interrupted them—a sound so faint they might have missed it if not for the sudden stillness that had fallen over them. They turned in unison toward a rock formation several yards away.

Emberstriker, the young dragonet Jorr had rescued weeks earlier, stumbled into view. Her movements were uncoordinated, almost drunken, her head weaving unsteadily.

"No," Jorr whispered.

The dragonet took another unsteady step before her legs seemed to give way beneath her. She collapsed onto her side, a pitiful whimper escaping her throat.

Pryce sprinted toward the fallen dragonet. He reached Emberstriker first, dropping to his knees beside her. The dragonet's breathing came in irregular gasps, her sides heaving with the effort.

"Jorr!" Pryce shouted, carefully placing a hand on Emberstriker's neck. "She's ice cold!"

Jorr appeared beside him. He gently pried open one of Emberstriker's eyes. The pupil appeared clouded and dilated.

"Limeroot poisoning," he confirmed. "It's affecting her nervous system already."

"Will she—" Pryce couldn't finish the question.

"Not if I can help it." Jorr ran his hands along the dragonet's body, checking vital points. "Kai, I need you to run to the upper spring—the one by the eastern volcanic vent. Bring back as much fresh water as you can carry."

Kai nodded once and took off at a run, his spear abandoned beside the cistern.

"What can I do?" Pryce asked, feeling helpless. Emberstriker's breathing seemed to grow more labored with each passing moment.

"Help me move her to the treatment shed," Jorr said. "Carefully. Her balance sensors are affected—any sudden movement will cause her distress."

Together they lifted the dragonet, who weighed more than her size suggested. Emberstriker released another weak hiss, her tail twitching involuntarily as they carried her.

"It's all right," Pryce said, unsure if the dragonet could understand him. "We've got you. You're going to be all right."

But as they laid Emberstriker on the padding of the treatment shed, Pryce wasn't certain he believed his own words. The dragonet's eyes had closed completely now, her breathing shallow and irregular. Her copper scales lay flat and dull against her skin.

"This wasn't meant to be discovered yet," Jorr said, already gathering herbs from storage containers built into the shed's walls. "The poisoner intended for all the dragons to consume the water over days, developing symptoms gradually. We weren't supposed to find out until it was too late."

"Emberstriker must have been drinking more than the others," Pryce said. "She's always been drawn to water."

Jorr nodded as he crushed leaves between stone mortar and pestle. "Young dragonets need more hydration than adults. And her smaller body size means the toxin affects her more quickly."

"Can you save her?" Pryce asked, unable to keep the fear from his voice.

Jorr paused in his work, his eyes meeting Pryce's. "I'm going to try. But we need to know who did this—and why they targeted the sanctuary."

The answer seemed all too clear to Pryce. As he stroked Emberstriker's neck, feeling each labored breath, his mind circled back to the same conclusion. The sanctuary wasn't just a refuge for injured dragons—it was a symbol of cooperation between Shorlings and Dragons. The kind of cooperation Thane seemed determined to destroy.

"I think I know," Pryce said quietly, as the dragonet shuddered beneath his touch. "And they're not finished yet."

***

Twilight settled over Emberfall. Inside the treatment shed, three figures moved in a desperate dance around the fallen dragonet. Hours had passed since they'd discovered Emberstriker's poisoning, each minute marked by her labored breathing and occasional whimpers that seemed to physically pain Jorr each time they escaped her throat.

"Hold her head steady," Jorr instructed, grinding another handful of dark leaves into paste. Sweat beaded on his brow despite the evening's cooling air. "She needs to swallow this without choking."

Pryce cradled the dragonet's head in his lap, fingers gently stroking the scales of her throat. "I've got her. She's not fighting as much now."

"That's not necessarily good," Jorr said. "The poison affects muscle control. Less struggle might mean deeper toxicity."

Kai burst through the door, water sloshing from two wooden buckets that had clearly been filled with haste. His face was flushed from repeated sprints up the volcanic slope to the clean spring.

"Sixth trip's the charm," he gasped, setting the buckets down carefully. "Though I'm fairly certain my arms will never forgive me."

Jorr mixed the fresh water with his herbal paste. The scent of crushed sulfur plants filled the small shed.

"These plants grow only around volcanic vents," he explained as he worked. "The minerals they absorb counteract certain toxins. My mentor taught me their uses when I first began training with dragons."

"What else do you need?" Pryce asked, watching Jorr add a pinch of crystalline powder to the mixture.

"Time. And that's the one thing we're short on."

Another weak tremor passed through Emberstriker's body. Her eyes opened briefly, before closing again.

"Here," Jorr said, passing a cloth soaked in the herbal mixture to Pryce. "Apply this to her throat scales—they'll absorb some of the medicine directly into her system."

Pryce worked carefully, dabbing the strong-smelling liquid along the dragonet's neck while Jorr prepared a more concentrated dose for oral administration. Kai busied himself cleaning the shed's stone floor, flushing away spilled water and scattered herbs.

"The water cistern?" Pryce asked, not looking up from his task.

"Drained completely," Kai said. "I diverted the collection pipes. Any new rainfall will bypass the contaminated basin."

"And the feed storage?"

"Sealed. Contaminated bags marked and separated."

Jorr nodded approvingly at Kai. "You have a natural instinct for dragon care."

"More like a natural instinct for crisis management," Kai said. "Growing up in a smithy teaches you how to handle burns, broken tools, and the occasional explosion. This is just . . . scaled up."

"Pryce," Jorr called, holding a small bowl of gloppy liquid. "I need you to tilt her head back slightly. Just enough for me to administer this."

Together they worked to position Emberstriker, Pryce supporting her neck while Jorr carefully opened her jaws. He trickled the medicine down her throat in small amounts, pausing between each to ensure she swallowed.

"That's it," Jorr said to the dragonet. "Fight it, little one."

Night had settled over the island. Stormwing appeared occasionally at the shed's small window, the storm dragon checking on them with concerned rumbles that vibrated the glass.

"She knows something's wrong," Pryce said, glancing toward the window.

"Dragons sense illness in their own," Jorr said. "Especially poisoning. It registers as . . . wrongness . . . to them."

Hours blurred together in a relentless cycle: preparing poultices, administering medicines, monitoring breathing, fetching fresh water. They moved around each other like a practiced team, anticipating needs before they were voiced.

"Hot compress for her chest," Jorr would say, and Kai would already be heating water.

"She's shivering again," Pryce would notice, and Jorr would reach for specific herbs without needing to be asked.

Midnight came and went. Emberstriker's breathing, which had been alarmingly shallow, gradually deepened. The clouding in her eyes began to clear when Jorr checked her pupils.

"The tremors are subsiding," Jorr said during one examination. "Her body is fighting back."

It was past three in the morning when Jorr finally sat back on his heels, exhausted. "She's stabilizing. Not out of danger yet, but the immediate crisis is passing."

Pryce realized he'd been holding his breath only when it escaped in a long exhale. "She'll recover?"

"With continued treatment, yes. Though it will take time for her to regain full strength."

Kai, who had been dozing against the wall between water runs, stirred at their voices. "Good news? Please tell me it's good news. My legs have forgotten what it feels like not to be climbing volcanic slopes."

"She's going to make it," Pryce told him.

They moved Emberstriker to a soft nest of clean bedding, positioning her where they could monitor her throughout the night. With the immediate danger passed, they finally stepped outside the treatment shed, their bodies crying out for rest.

Jorr built a small fire near the shed's entrance. They sat in a rough circle, none wanting to stray far from Emberstriker even though she now slept peacefully.

"This wasn't random," Pryce said after a long silence, staring into the flames. "Someone knew exactly what they were doing."

"Dragonkin knowledge," Jorr agreed. "The poison, the sabotage points—all of it shows familiarity with dragon handling."

"Thane," Kai said flatly. "Has to be. This fits his pattern perfectly."

"But why target the sanctuary?" Jorr asked. "These dragons are no threat to anyone. Many are still recovering from injuries."

"Because it's something I care about," Pryce said. "Something all of us care about. And because it represents cooperation between Shorlings and Dragonkin—the very thing Thane seems determined to destroy."

The fire crackled between them, sparks spiraling upward to join the stars that blanketed Emberfall's night sky.

"He's methodical," Kai said. "First undermining you in the village, then targeting the sanctuary. What's next?"

"I don't know," Pryce said. "But I'm not waiting to find out."

Jorr added another small branch to the fire. "Whatever happens, the sanctuary needs protection. These dragons can't defend themselves, especially now."

"Let's make a pact," Pryce said, meeting first Jorr's eyes, then Kai's. "Thane wants to divide us— Shorling from Dragonkin, friend from friend. We don't let him."

Kai extended his hand across the fire. "Together, then. For the dragons, for Crystal Shores, for all of it."

Jorr placed his scaled hand atop Kai's. "Together."

Pryce completed the circle, his hand joining theirs. The touch seemed to seal something between them as Emberstriker released a soft chirp in her sleep.

CHAPTER 9

Stormwing descended through the morning mist as Crystal Shores emerged below them.

"There's more smoke than usual from the chimneys," Kai said from behind him, pointing toward the village. "And look at the harbor—twice as many Dragonkin ships as when we left."

Pryce guided Stormwing toward their usual landing spot on the bluff overlooking the village. "One Day at Emberfall felt like a vacation. Now back to reality."

They'd left Jorr with strict instructions for Emberstriker's continued recovery, along with new security measures for the sanctuary. The young dragonet had been recovering when they departed, though still weak from the limeroot poisoning.

After dismounting, Pryce gave Stormwing an affectionate pat on her neck. "Rest up, girl. Something tells me we're going to need you again soon."

The dragon snorted. She settled onto her haunches, watching as Pryce and Kai made their way down the winding path toward the village.

"Faye sent an urgent message while we were at Emberfall," Pryce said, pulling a crumpled note from his pocket. "Something about troubling replies from the villages."

"Knowing Faye, 'urgent' probably means the end of the world as we know it," Kai said. "She gets that from your mother—the Harper women don't panic over small things."

They found their way to Faye's secondary message center in the village, passing through streets that felt subtly different than when they'd left. Pryce noticed more Dragonkin guards on patrol, their scaled faces watched every passerby. Conversations seemed to stop when he walked by, replaced by whispers and sideways glances.

"Popular as ever," Kai said under his breath. "I'll join you shortly, Pryce. I want to check on my family."

The morning sun slanted through the latticed windows of Faye's message center, casting geometric shadows across the rows of sorting cubbies. Pryce found his sister hunched over her desk, her red curls escaping their braid as she frowned at a collection of rolled parchments.

"You sent for me?" Pryce asked, closing the door behind him as gulls rustled in their perches.

Faye looked up, relieved at the sight of him. "Thank the lake you're back. The replies from yesterday's message run are . . . strange." She gestured to three neatly arranged piles of correspondence. "Hostile. All of them."

Pryce approached the desk. "Hostile how?"

"See for yourself." Faye handed him a letter bearing the official seal of Fernmoor. "This is from Mayor Aldrich. We've sent them weather warnings for years without issue."

Pryce unrolled the parchment and read aloud:

"Crystal Shores' presumptuous warnings are no longer welcome. Perhaps your new Dragonkin masters have filled your heads with delusions of authority over neighboring villages. Fernmoor requires no guidance from a settlement that surrenders its autonomy to scaled invaders."

"Scaled invaders," Pryce repeated.

"That's just the beginning." Faye handed him another letter, this one from Millhaven. "Same tone, different words. They're all questioning your authority, suggesting Crystal Shores has been 'compromised by foreign influence.'"

Pryce scanned the Millhaven correspondence:

"Reports reach us of a young leader more concerned with appeasing Dragonkin nobility than protecting Shorling interests. Perhaps it is time the coastal villages reconsidered their alliances."

"And this one," Faye said, producing a third letter, "from Rushwater. Listen to this: *'We cannot trust intelligence from a village whose council seat is held by one bearing the marks of Dragonkin transformation.'"*

Pryce's hand moved reflexively to his jawline, where the faint scales still marked him. "They mention the scales specifically?"

"Many of them. Pryce, these villages have known you since you were a child. Some of these mayors watched you learn to sail. They wouldn't write such things unprompted."

Kai appeared in the doorway. "The harbor's buzzing with talk about letters," he said, stepping inside. "Traders are refusing to unload cargo, claiming they don't want to risk 'association with a Dragonkin puppet state.'"

"Someone's been writing to them," Pryce said, handing the letters to Kai. "Someone who knows enough about our situation to make their lies convincing."

Kai scanned the notes. "This isn't random gossip. Look at the phrasing—'presumptuous warnings,' 'compromised by foreign influence,' 'marks of Dragonkin transformation.' These are coordinated. Someone with inside knowledge is feeding them information."

Faye stood and moved to a large map of Lake Dragontide pinned to the wall. Colored threads connected Crystal Shores to various coastal settlements. "I track every message we send and receive. Look at the timing." She pointed to small notations beside each thread. "All these hostile replies came in response to messages we sent three days ago—routine weather reports and trade updates."

"But someone reached these villages before our messages," Pryce said, understanding dawning. "Someone who knew exactly what we were going to say."

"More than that," Kai added, studying the letters. "Someone who could forge official seals. These aren't casual letters from concerned mayors—they're formal diplomatic correspondence. That requires resources."

Faye nodded. "And access to our outgoing message logs. Whoever's doing this knew precisely which villages to target and what topics each mayor was concerned with."

"Thane," Pryce said.

"Can we prove it?" Kai asked.

"Not yet. But who else has the resources, the access, and the motive?"

A soft tapping at the window interrupted them. Skye perched on the sill, a message capsule attached to her leg. Faye opened the window, and the bird hopped inside.

Faye removed the capsule. "Should be returning from Thornwick with confirmation of grain shipments."

As Faye unrolled the message, her face grew pale. "Thornwick's mayor writes that he's 'reconsidering trade agreements' with Crystal

Shores. Says he's received 'disturbing intelligence' about our village's new loyalties."

"That's the seventh village," Faye continued. "Fernmoor, Millhaven, Rushwater, Ashford, Greenvale, Saltmere, and now Thornwick. Pryce, this isn't just undermining your authority—this is isolation."

Pryce moved to the window, staring out at Crystal Shores' harbor where Dragonkin and Shorling vessels bobbed side by side. "If the surrounding villages refuse to trade with us, refuse to share intelligence about Corsair movements—"

"Crystal Shores becomes an island," Faye finished. "Completely dependent on Dragonkin support."

"Which gives Queen Nymeria an excuse to establish a permanent presence here," Kai added. "For our 'protection,' of course."

Pryce felt his chest tighten as the implications became clear. "Thane's not just trying to discredit me personally. He's orchestrating Crystal Shores' political isolation to justify Dragonkin occupation."

"But we need proof," Faye said. "Something more concrete than suspicions."

Kai cracked his knuckles, a habit that always preceded his more questionable suggestions. "Then we need to catch him in the act. Find out how he's sending these letters, who's helping him—"

"And how he's getting information about our outgoing messages," Pryce added. "Someone inside Crystal Shores is feeding him intelligence."

Faye moved to a cabinet near her desk, withdrawing a leather-bound ledger. "I log every message that goes out, every messenger who comes in. If someone's been accessing this information, there might be clues."

She opened the book, revealing pages of detailed entries. "Here—the day Thane arrived. Normal activity until . . ." She paused, finger tracing a line of text. "Someone requested access to the message logs that evening. Official council business, the note says."

"Who made the request?" Pryce asked.

"No signature. Just a general council authorization stamp." Faye's frown deepened. "That stamp should only be used for emergency access. I remember wondering about it, but there was so much chaos with Thane's arrival—"

"The same day Thane arrived," Kai said. "Not a coincidence."

"We need to follow the trail of these letters," Pryce said. "Find out how they're being sent, who's carrying them. Thane's too smart to use our official messenger service."

"The merchant quarter," Faye said. "Traders carry letters between villages all the time. Less official than the messenger service, harder to track."

"Good thinking. Kai, you know the merchants better than I do—"

A shadow passed by the window, followed by a soft rustling sound. Then another. The gulls in their perches began chattering.

"What's gotten into them?" Kai asked, glancing at the restless birds.

Faye moved to the window, peering out. "Something spooked them. But I don't see—"

A small object bounced off the glass with a soft clink. Then another. Tiny pebbles, apparently thrown from below.

"Someone's trying to get our attention," Pryce said, moving to join Faye at the window.

In the narrow alley behind the message center, a figure stood partially hidden behind a stack of barrels. The patchwork cloak was unmistakable— just as his mother had described, it seemed to hold pieces of a dozen different travelers' garments, all stitched together.

"Pipwhistle," Pryce said, the Quibnocket his mother had spoken of so often.

The figure below urgently pointed toward the main street, then melted back into the shadows with the grace of someone accustomed to avoiding notice.

"Did you just say Pipwhistle?" Faye asked, wide-eyed. "Mother's Pipwhistle? The one from her stories?"

"Unless there's another Quibnocket in Crystal Shores." Pryce said. "He helped mother once. Maybe he's trying to help us now."

"Or maybe it's a trap," Kai said, already reaching for his spear.

"Pipwhistle doesn't trap people," Faye said firmly. "Mother always said Quibnockets might meddle and steal, but they don't betray trusts."

"One way to find out." Pryce opened the door, then paused. "Faye, keep checking those message logs. Look for anyone who's had access in the past week. We'll follow Pipwhistle, see what he's trying to show us."

"Be careful," Faye called after them. "And remember—mother said Pipwhistle communicates in riddles. Don't expect straightforward answers."

They made their way quickly through Crystal Shores' narrow streets, following glimpses of patchwork cloak that always seemed to stay just ahead of them. Pipwhistle led them through a maze of alleys and side streets, avoiding the main thoroughfares where Dragonkin guards maintained their patrols.

"He's taking us toward the merchant quarter," Kai said as they turned down a street lined with trading stalls and warehouses.

"Toward the Dragon's Rest Inn," Pryce corrected, recognizing the building ahead. "That's where most of the traveling merchants stay when they're in Crystal Shores."

Pipwhistle paused at the corner of a warehouse, waiting for them to catch up. As they approached, he held up a finger to his lips, then pointed around the corner toward the inn's side entrance.

Pryce peered carefully around the building's edge. In the inn's small courtyard, Thane stood speaking with a man in traveler's clothing—a merchant from his dress, though his bearing suggested more than simple trade business.

"...must be distributed within two days," Thane was saying, his voice carrying clearly in the still air. "The northern villages first, then the eastern settlements. Timing is crucial."

The merchant nodded, accepting a small leather satchel from Thane. "And the payment arrangements?"

"Your usual fee, plus a bonus for discretion." Thane smiled. "Remember—these letters must appear to be routine trade correspondence. No one should suspect their true origin."

"Of course, Battlemaster. My men have been carrying such 'trade letters' for years. We know how to avoid unwanted attention."

Pryce felt Kai tense beside him. This was the proof they'd been seeking—Thane actively coordinating the letter campaign against Crystal Shores.

Pipwhistle tugged at Pryce's sleeve, pointing toward a small window on the inn's second floor.

Through it, they could see into a room where several more merchants waited, each with their own collection of letters and packages.

"A whole network," Kai whispered.

The merchant below was preparing to leave when Pipwhistle suddenly stepped into the courtyard, bold as daylight, his hands already moving with the sleight-of-hand of a master pickpocket.

"Excuse me, good ser," Pipwhistle called in a voice like tinkling bells, approaching the merchant with an exaggerated stumble. "Might you spare a coin for a poor traveler? The roads have been unkind to these old bones."

The merchant recoiled slightly from the eccentric figure, but before he could respond, Pipwhistle had somehow relieved him of the leather satchel Thane had given him, the bag quickly vanishing into the Quibnocket's voluminous cloak.

"Here now!" Thane shouted, recognizing the theft. "Stop him!"

But Pipwhistle was already moving, darting between stacked barrels with the agility of someone a third his apparent age. The merchant gave chase, with Thane close behind, their shouts echoing off the warehouse walls.

"That's our cue," Pryce said, pulling Kai back from the corner. "He's given us what we need—now let's not waste it."

They slipped away through the alleys, taking a circuitous route back to the message center. Only when they were safely inside did they realize Pipwhistle had somehow arrived before them, sitting calmly on a windowsill as if he'd been there all along.

"Ah, young Pryce," Pipwhistle said, his voice carrying an amused lilt. "Your mother spoke truly—you have her eyes for truth and her backbone for justice."

The Quibnocket tossed the stolen satchel to Pryce. "Letters written in Thane's hand, sealed with false signatures, and addressed to six different village mayors. Each one designed to further isolate Crystal Shores from its neighbors."

Kai shook his head in amazement. "How did you—?"

"Questions are like fish nets, young Frostborne—cast too wide, and you catch mostly water." Pipwhistle grinned. "The real question is: what will you do with the proof you now possess?"

Pryce opened the satchel, finding exactly what Pipwhistle had described—draft letters in what had to be Thane's handwriting, each one written to inflame a specific village's concerns about Crystal Shores' Dragonkin alliance.

"Take these to Princess Seren," Pryce said to Faye. "She needs to see what Thane's been doing."

"And what about you?" Faye asked.

"We're going back to watch Thane's reaction when he realizes he has lost the messages. Angry people make mistakes."

Pipwhistle chuckled, already moving toward the window. "Before you go charging off like young heroes, remember this—Thane Zharan is more than he appears. His father's disgrace runs deeper than family shame. Ask yourselves: what would drive a battlemaster to such elaborate schemes?"

"What do you know about his father?" Pryce asked, but Pipwhistle was already climbing out the window.

"Stories within stories, young ones. Truth wrapped in secrets, wrapped in lies." Then he disappeared into the afternoon shadows. "But beware—when cornered, even lesser dragons grow dangerous."

Kai adjusted his spear across his shoulders. "Right now, we need to get back to that inn. Thane will be furious about those missing letters, and fury makes people careless."

As they prepared to leave, Faye called after them. "Pryce! The message logs—I found something. Someone's been making copies of our outgoing correspondence for the past six days. The handwriting . . . it's not one of ours."

Faye spread Thane's stolen letters across her desk, and read each one. The systematic nature of the deception was even worse than they'd suspected—Thane hadn't just been undermining

Pryce's reputation, he'd been laying the groundwork for Crystal Shores' complete diplomatic isolation.

"Keep that information safe," Pryce said. "We'll need it when we confront Thane publicly."

They slipped back into Crystal Shores' winding streets, moving toward the merchant quarter where an increasingly desperate battlemaster would soon discover that his carefully orchestrated campaign had been thoroughly compromised.

But now they had proof. And proof, as Pipwhistle had implied, was a weapon that cut both ways.

The question was: how would Thane react when he realized his plans had been exposed?

CHAPTER 10

Seren had grown accustomed to Crystal Shores' peculiar rhythm—the morning bustle of fishing boats departing, the midday quiet as villagers sought shade, the evening gatherings that turned strangers into storytellers. Standing on the balcony of the guest quarters assigned to her delegation, she watched Shorling children chase each other through the square below, their laughter carrying on the warm breeze.

For the first time since arriving, Crystal Shores felt almost peaceful. Almost like a place she could—

"Your Highness."

Seren turned to find Commander Drakonir approaching with haste.

"What is it, Commander?"

"A ship approaches from the east. Bearing Her Majesty's personal standard."

"My mother? Here?"

"The harbormaster's confirmed it. Queen Nymeria's flagship, with a full escort of three vessels. They'll dock within the hour."

Her mother's visits were never unexpected—they were calculated. Every surprise arrival served a purpose, usually one that left others scrambling to accommodate royal whims while Nymeria observed their reactions like a predator.

"Summon my guards. Full ceremonial dress. And send word to Mayor Wright—tell her Queen Nymeria requests an immediate audience with the joint council."

"Requests, Your Highness?"

"Demands, then. My mother doesn't request anything."

As Drakonir departed, Seren remained on the balcony, watching the distant speck of her mother's ship grow larger against the horizon. The warm afternoon suddenly felt oppressive.

***

The Great Hall had been hastily prepared for royal reception, though Seren knew her mother would find fault with something—the placement of chairs, the quality of refreshments, the presumption of treating her as an equal to Mayor Wright rather than the sovereign she considered herself.

Seren took her position at the right hand of the hastily erected throne Mayor Wright had ordered brought from storage—an ancient Shorling ceremonial seat that looked modest beside the grandeur Nymeria was accustomed to. Around the hall, Dragonkin and Shorling representatives arranged themselves according to negotiated protocols.

Pryce entered with Kai at his side, both young men looking uncomfortable in formal attire.

"Nervous?" Kai asked quietly.

"Terrified," Pryce admitted, adjusting his formal vest as he looked at Seren. "Your mother arriving unannounced usually means someone's about to have a very bad day."

Before Seren could respond, the great doors swung open. Queen Nymeria entered with the fluid grace of a predator, her midnight blue cloak flowing behind her. Her silver eyes swept the assembly.

Behind her came Battlemaster Thane.

"Your Majesty," Mayor Wright said, rising and offering a formal bow. "Crystal Shores welcomes you."

"Mayor Wright." Nymeria's voice carried the musical quality common among nobility. "I thought it prudent to inspect this alliance personally. Reports from the field can be . . . incomplete."

She settled onto the throne with casual authority, her gaze finding Seren. "My daughter. You look well. Country air, perhaps?"

"Thank you, Mother. The alliance progresses favorably."

"Does it?" Nymeria's attention shifted to Pryce, studying him with the intensity of a dragon examining potential prey. "Young Harper-Green. I understand you've assumed responsibilities beyond your years in your parents' absence."

"I serve Crystal Shores as needed, Your Majesty."

"Indeed. And how fares your dragon training? I'm told Stormwing has become quite formidable under your guidance."

Something in her mother's tone raised warning bells in Seren's mind. The question seemed casual, but Nymeria never asked casual questions.

"Stormwing and I work well together," Pryce replied.

"Excellent." Nymeria smiled. "Battlemaster Thane has provided detailed reports of your . . . leadership style. Most illuminating."

Seren watched Thane step forward slightly.

"Your Majesty is too kind," Thane said with perfect humility. "I've merely observed and advised where appropriate."

"And your observations?"

"The young councilor shows promise, though perhaps lacks the experience such troubled times demand. The recent training incident, the tavern altercation—understandable mistakes for one so young."

Seren saw Pryce's hands clench at his sides.

"Indeed. Youth often brings passion where experience would counsel restraint. Still, the boy has proven useful in maintaining this alliance, wouldn't you agree, Battlemaster?"

"Absolutely, Your Majesty. Though I confess concern about the Corsair threat. Perhaps more experienced leadership might better coordinate our joint defenses."

Mayor Wright cleared her throat. "Your Majesty, if I may—young Harper-Green has shown remarkable capability in managing our alliance protocols. His actions have consistently demonstrated—"

"Have they?" Nymeria's eyes fixed on the mayor. "I understand there were difficulties during a recent training exercise. Guards injured, protocols confused?"

Seren felt ice forming in her stomach. Her mother knew details she shouldn't possess—unless those details had been provided by someone present.

"Training exercises involve inherent risks, Your Majesty," Pryce said. "We learn from every experience."

"How admirable. Though I wonder—do such learning experiences serve Crystal Shores' defense needs? With Corsairs in the region, can mistakes be afforded?"

Seren watched her mother's performance with growing unease. Every word was calculated to undermine Pryce while appearing supportive of the alliance itself.

"Perhaps," Nymeria continued, "Battlemaster Thane might share his expertise more directly. Coordinate training protocols, oversee joint operations—ensure the alliance achieves its full potential."

"An honor I would gladly accept," Thane replied smoothly.

Seren saw Kai's hand move subtly toward his spear, while Pryce remained motionless.

"Your Majesty," Seren said, "the current arrangements have proven effective. Perhaps disrupting established protocols might—"

"My dear," Nymeria's voice carried a warning wrapped in maternal affection, "surely you don't question the wisdom of optimizing our alliance's effectiveness?"

"Of course not, Mother. I merely suggest that hasty changes might introduce complications."

Nymeria studied her daughter. "Experience will guide us. Battlemaster Thane, you will remain in Crystal Shores to provide such guidance as circumstances require."

"As you command, Your Majesty."

The formal session continued for another hour, with Nymeria dispensing royal pronouncements that systematically expanded Dragonkin authority within Crystal Shores' existing structures. By the time she dismissed the assembly, the balance of power had shifted significantly—though subtly enough that open protest would seem petty.

As the hall emptied, Seren lingered, watching her mother converse quietly with Thane and several Dragonkin commanders.

"Princess Seren?"

She turned to find Pryce approaching.

"Walk with me," she said quietly. "The gardens. Away from listening ears."

They made their way through Crystal Shores' modest gardens—a collection of carefully tended plots behind the Great Hall where villagers grew herbs and vegetables. Compared to Drakemere's elaborate royal gardens, they seemed humble, but Seren found their practical beauty oddly appealing.

"Your mother made her position clear," Pryce said once they were safely alone among the bean rows and herb patches.

"She made Thane's position clear," Seren corrected. "He's not here as an advisor, Pryce. He's here as her representative. Her eyes and voice."

"And you? What's your position in all this?"

Seren paused beside a patch of lake mint, its scent sharp and clean in the afternoon air. "I'm beginning to think I don't know anymore."

"What did she mean about reports from Thane? What kind of details has he been providing?"

The question Seren had been dreading. "Everything, I suspect. Your movements, your meetings, your decisions. She knew about the training incident in detail no public report would contain."

"How is that possible? Those details would only be known to people present—"

"Or people with access to those who were present." Seren picked a sprig of mint, crushing it between her fingers. "Thane arrived the same day the incident occurred. Yet my mother spoke as if she'd had full reports for days."

"You think Thane's been reporting to her since before he arrived?"

"I think Thane's been in communication with her far longer than any of us realized. I think this entire alliance might be proceeding exactly as she planned."

Pryce was quiet for a long moment, his gaze following a butterfly that danced between the garden rows.

"The betrothal," he said finally. "Was that part of the plan too?"

Seren felt guilt, regret. "I thought it was spontaneous. A diplomatic solution to a crisis. But now . . ."

"Now you think she orchestrated the crisis to create the need for a solution?"

"I don't know what to think anymore." The admission felt like stepping off a cliff. "Everything I believed about this alliance, about my role here, about her intentions—it's all shifting under my feet."

They walked deeper into the gardens, past tomato vines and rows of onions, until they reached a small stone bench beside a miniature pond that reflected the sky.

"There's something else," Seren said, settling on the bench. "Something Thane said to the other commanders while you were speaking with Mayor Wright."

"What?"

"He mentioned timeline adjustments. Said phase one was proceeding ahead of schedule, and they might need to accelerate phase two."

Pryce sat beside her. "Phases of what?"

"That's what I need to find out." Seren turned to face him fully. "Pryce, I need you to understand something. When I agreed to this betrothal, I believed I was preventing a war. I thought I was choosing the lesser evil for both our peoples."

"And now?"

"Now I think I might have been a pawn in starting one."

Seren realized this might be the first genuine conversation she'd had since arriving in Crystal Shores—certainly the first where she wasn't performing a role dictated by duty and diplomacy.

"So what do we do?" Pryce asked.

"We find out what my mother and Thane are really planning. And we decide whether our betrothal serves their goals or ours."

A movement near the garden's entrance caught Seren's attention. Thane stood there, partially concealed by a trellis of flowering vines, clearly observing them. When he realized he'd been spotted, he smiled and approached with his usual confident stride.

"Your Highness, Councilor Harper-Green," he said with a formal bow. "Enjoying the local flora?"

"The gardens are quite charming," Seren replied. "We were discussing arrangements for tomorrow's joint patrol schedule."

"Ah, excellent. I was hoping to review those protocols myself. Her Majesty has specific requirements for coordination procedures."

Seren stood, brushing stone grit from her dress. "Of course, Battlemaster. I'll ensure you receive full briefings."

As they walked back toward the Great Hall, Seren caught Pryce's eye briefly. In that glance, she tried to convey everything she couldn't say aloud: that his suspicions about Thane were correct, that her mother's arrival boded ill for Crystal Shores, and that their betrothal had just become far more complicated than a simple diplomatic arrangement.

***

Evening found Seren in her mother's private tent, erected in the courtyard of the building housing the Dragonkin delegation. The space was a masterwork of controlled opulence—rich fabrics, elegant furnishings, and subtle display of power that reminded everyone of Nymeria's rank without appearing grandiose to Shorling sensibilities.

"You seem troubled, my dear," Nymeria said, pouring wine into two goblets. The liquid was deep crimson, imported from the southern volcanic islands that formed the heart of Dragonkin territory.

"The day has been . . . eventful," Seren replied, accepting the goblet her mother offered.

"Indeed. Crystal Shores proves more complex than anticipated. Tell me, what is your assessment of young Harper-Green?"

Seren sipped her wine, tasting sulfur and dark berries. "He's intelligent. Dedicated. Perhaps naive about political realities."

"Naive. Yes, that's the impression Battlemaster Thane conveys as well." Nymeria settled into her chair, the picture of maternal concern. "It troubles me to see you bound to someone so . . . unprepared for the challenges ahead."

"The betrothal serves its political purpose, Mother. Personal compatibility is secondary."

"Is it?" Nymeria looked at her daughter with uncomfortable intensity. "Because recent reports

149

suggest you've grown quite comfortable here. Perhaps too comfortable."

Seren felt her scales shift subtly. "I've fulfilled my duties exactly as instructed."

"Have you? Thane mentions you've been spending considerable time with the boy. Walks in gardens, private conversations, defending his decisions in council."

"I'm meant to appear supportive of the alliance. Surely some interaction is expected?"

Nymeria set down her goblet. "Seren, this engagement is a tool—a means to legitimize our eventual absorption of Crystal Shores into our territory. You haven't forgotten that, have you?"

"Absorption?"

"Did you truly think we would maintain this charade indefinitely? Crystal Shores has strategic value—its location, its dragon-handling facilities, its position controlling the northern trade routes . . . and the dragon ore beneath our feet. The Corsair threat merely provides convenient justification for what was always inevitable."

Seren struggled to keep her voice steady. "And the people of Crystal Shores? They believe this is a genuine alliance."

"They believe what they need to believe. Once we've established permanent garrisons here, once Dragonkin law supersedes their provincial councils, they'll adapt. They always do."

"And my betrothal to Pryce?"

Nymeria smiled—the expression Seren had learned to fear as a child. "Once the transition is complete, such arrangements become . . . negotiable. Young Harper-Green will either prove useful to our administration or find himself retired to private life. Either way, your future lies elsewhere."

The tent felt suffocating. Seren fought the urge to flee. "You planned this from the beginning. The Corsair attacks, Thane's arrival, everything."

"I planned to protect Dragonkin interests, as is my duty as queen. If that required creating circumstances favorable to our goals, so be it."

A soft rustling at the tent's entrance interrupted them. Thane appeared, offering a respectful bow.

"Your Majesty, forgive the intrusion. The evening reports are ready for your review."

"Excellent timing, Battlemaster. Join us— Seren was just expressing concern about the . . . complexity of our arrangements here."

Thane entered fully, settling into a chair with an ease that spoke of frequent private audiences with the queen.

"The girl has performed admirably," he said, though his tone suggested criticism lay beneath the praise. "Though I wonder if extended exposure to Shorling sentiment might be affecting her judgment."

"Explain."

Seren watched in horrified fascination as Thane recounted details of her interactions with Pryce—conversations she'd thought private, moments of apparent cooperation, her defense of decisions that aligned with Crystal Shores' interests rather than pure Dragonkin advantage.

"She's maintained the facade perfectly," Thane concluded. "But recent behavior suggests emotional investment that could complicate final implementation."

"Emotional investment," Nymeria repeated, her gaze fixing on Seren. "Is this accurate?"

"I've grown to understand their perspective," Seren said. "Such understanding serves our diplomatic goals."

"Understanding, yes. Sympathy, however, can become problematic." Nymeria leaned forward slightly. "Tell me, daughter—if circumstances required immediate action against Crystal Shores' current leadership, would personal feelings interfere with your duties?"

Seren understood the test implicit in her mother's words—declare absolute loyalty to Dragonkin interests, or be deemed compromised.

"My duties to our people remain paramount," she said.

"Good." Nymeria smiled. "Because circumstances are accelerating. The Corsair fleet will arrive soon, and when they do, we must be prepared to act decisively."

"Act how?" Seren asked, though she dreaded the answer.

Thane spoke before Nymeria could respond. "The Corsair assault will test Crystal Shores' defenses severely. Their current leadership may prove . . . inadequate . . . to the challenge. Should casualties remove certain individuals from their positions, we'll be ready to step in. To restore order."

"Casualties," Seren repeated.

"War is unpredictable," Nymeria said. "Even allies can find themselves in unexpected danger when battle is joined."

The tent seemed to close in around Seren as the full scope of their plan became clear. Not just occupation, but calculated elimination of anyone who might resist Dragonkin rule. And Pryce, with his growing leadership among the villagers, would certainly be seen as a threat.

"I should retire," Seren said. "Tomorrow will require early preparation."

"Indeed. Sleep well, daughter. Soon our work here will be complete."

Seren managed to reach her own quarters before her composure finally cracked. She sank onto her bed, staring at the ceiling while her mother's words echoed in her mind. *Emotional investment. Casualties. Final implementation.*

She thought of Pryce's earnest attempts to bridge the gap between their peoples, his genuine care for both Shorling and Dragonkin under his protection. She remembered his fury when Thane had insulted Stormwing—the loyalty that had driven him to violence in defense of what he loved.

And she realized that somewhere between diplomatic ceremony and garden conversations, she had indeed developed emotional investment. The question now was whether she would let that investment doom the young man whose only crime was trying to save his people.

The war for Crystal Shores' future would be fought on multiple fronts. And Seren had just chosen her side.

CHAPTER 11

Pryce stood atop the watchtower overlooking Tremor Point as twilight fell over Lake Dragontide. Thunder rumbled in the distance, promising a storm that would complicate any nocturnal activities. Beside him, Kai adjusted the strap of his spear while scanning the horizon through a battered spyglass.

"Still nothing," Kai said, lowering the instrument. "You'd think Corsairs would have the courtesy to attack during reasonable hours."

Pryce smiled. "I'll send them a strongly worded letter about proper raiding etiquette."

Below them, the defenses they'd spent days preparing stood ready—spiked rafts bobbing near the breakwater, lantern buoys marking safe channels, and the Tempest Guardian positioned to protect the harbor mouth. Dragonkin and Shorling forces maintained their scheduled watch rotations, though the tension between the groups remained.

"There," Pryce said suddenly, pointing northwest. "Movement on the water."

Kai raised the spyglass again, searching. "I see them. Three vessels, maybe four. Moving without lights."

"Scout ships," Pryce said. "Testing our defenses, seeing how we respond." He whistled to where Stormwing waited on a rocky outcropping. The storm dragon lifted her massive head.

"Signal the others," Pryce said to the lightkeeper. "All forces to ready positions."

The lighthouse signal fire blazed to life, its coded flashes alerting the village and harbor defenses. Within minutes, the organized chaos of preparation filled Crystal Shores—boats pushing off from docks, guards running to positions, families retreating to shelters.

Pryce vaulted onto Stormwing's back, quickly pulling his bow and quiver from their saddle attachments to sling them over his back. Kai scrambled up behind him.

"Remember," Pryce shouted over the wind as they climbed into the darkening sky, "we observe first. Find out what they're planning before we engage."

But even as he said it, the first crossbow bolt hissed past them—too close. These weren't just scouts.

"So much for observation," Kai said, gripping his spear tighter. "I count six ships now, not four."

Stormwing banked sharply as more projectiles sliced through the air around them. Her electrical field crackled, illuminating the approaching Corsair vessels. Black hulls, crimson sails, and the distinctive silhouette of weapons designed for killing dragons rather than piercing ship hulls.

"Pryce!" Kai pointed toward the harbor. "Look at our formations!"

Below them, the carefully coordinated defense positions had dissolved into confusion. Dragonkin war-dragons circled high above the bay, while Shorling forces manned their boats closer to shore. Between them, a gap had opened—precisely where the Corsair ships were heading.

"That's not right," Pryce said, recognizing the tactical error immediately. "The dragons should be supporting the naval forces, not flying independent patterns."

A horn blast echoed across the water—Thane's signal. Pryce watched in growing alarm as the Dragonkin dragons responded by climbing even higher, their formation spreading wider. Whatever orders Thane had given, they were pulling aerial support away from where it was most needed.

Stormwing dove toward the lead Corsair vessel, her presence alone causing several raiders to scramble for cover. But as they approached attack range, another horn blast sounded—different in pitch and rhythm.

"Pull back!" Thane's voice carried across the water. "Maintain elevation! Do not engage until the Shorling forces are clear!"

"Clear of what?" Kai shouted.

Pryce realized Thane's strategy. By keeping the dragons high and the boats low, he was creating a crossfire situation. Any attack would risk hitting their own allies.

"Signal lamp from the Tempest Guardian," Kai called, pointing toward the lone Oceanrider vessel. "Corrin's requesting dragon support at the harbor mouth."

But even as Pryce turned Stormwing toward the embattled ship, another Dragonkin dragon swept past them—close enough that the wind from its wings sent Stormwing tumbling.

"Watch your flight path!" the other rider shouted. "Battlemaster's orders—maintain formation!"

"What formation?" Pryce shouted, but the dragon was already climbing away.

The scene below descended into chaos. The Tempest Guardian exchanged cannon fire with two Corsair vessels while fishing boats laden with armed villagers tried to flank the enemy ships. Dragonkin forces circled overhead, their riders clearly frustrated but following Thane's contradictory orders.

"There!" Kai pointed toward Tremor Point's rocky beaches. "Landing boats!"

Three smaller Corsair vessels had slipped past the main battle, heading for the isolated beach where Old Man Doyle kept his prized goat herd. The animals bleated in terror as armed raiders stormed the narrow strand.

"We can't leave them," Pryce said, guiding Stormwing into a steep dive.

They swooped low over the beach, Stormwing's electrical discharge sending two Corsairs sprawling. But more raiders poured from the boats, driving the terrified goats toward a makeshift pen they'd erected on the sand.

"They're not raiding," Kai realized. "They're taking hostages. Live bait."

Old Man Doyle stumbled from his cottage, brandishing a shepherd's crook against the invaders. A Corsair raised his sword—

Lightning split the sky, but not from Stormwing. Another dragon descended from the storm clouds, its rider loosing a controlled blast that sent the raiders scattering. Princess Seren's dragon wheeled overhead, its shadow passing over the beach.

"Princess!" Pryce called out. "What are your orders?"

Seren looked toward the main battle, then back at the stranded villagers. For a moment, Pryce saw her indecision. Then she banked sharply, diving toward the Corsairs threatening Doyle.

"Protect the civilians!" she shouted. "I'll take the left flank!"

Together they drove the raiders back toward their boats, Stormwing and Seren's dragon working in coordination. But their success was short-lived. A horn blast from the main battle demanded all Dragonkin forces return to formation immediately.

Seren hesitated, looking between the fleeing Corsairs and the signal. "I have to—"

"Go," Pryce said. "I've got this."

But as Seren's dragon climbed away, more Corsair reinforcements appeared. Not boats this time—a full seadrake, its massive form cutting through the water like a living warship.

"By the depths," Kai said. "Look at the size of that thing."

The seadrake's roar echoed across the bay, a sound that seemed to freeze every defender in place. Its scales were black as midnight, marked with scars from countless battles. Chains and barbs adorned its harness, and astride its neck rode a Corsair captain.

"Pryce!" Old Man Doyle's voice cracked across the beach. "Help!"

The old man had tried to save one of his goats, but a Corsair spear had found its mark. He clutched his shoulder, bright blood seeping between his fingers as raiders advanced on his position.

Stormwing needed no urging. She plunged toward the beach, talons extended. But the angle was wrong—too steep, too fast. Pryce tried to adjust their approach, pulling up to avoid civilian casualties, when he heard it.

A horn blast. Not Dragonkin, not Shorling. Corsair.

The seadrake responded immediately, surging forward with speed. Directly beneath them, its jaws snapped closed with enough force to shatter ship masts.

Stormwing twisted desperately, but the seadrake's tail whipped from the water, catching her left wing. The impact sent them spinning, plummeting toward the rocky shore of Tremor Point.

"Hold on!" Pryce shouted, fighting to regain control.

They hit the beach hard, Stormwing rolling to absorb the impact while Pryce and Kai tumbled free. Sand and gravel sprayed around them as the dragon struggled to her feet, favoring her injured wing.

"Can she fly?" Kai asked, blood trickling from a cut on his forehead.

Stormwing spread her wings experimentally, then folded them with a grunt of pain. Not broken, but damaged enough to ground them.

Around them, the battle raged on. The Tempest Guardian had managed to sink one Corsair vessel, but two more pressed their attack. Dragonkin dragons finally descended to engage, but their coordination was chaotic, their timing off. Worst of all, Pryce could see Shorling boats caught in the crossfire as friendly forces nearly collided in the dark.

"This is a disaster," he said, watching a fishing boat veer wildly to avoid a diving dragon, only to sail directly into a Corsair broadside.

The explosion lit the night sky. When the smoke cleared, the boat was gone.

"No!" Doyle's voice broke with anguish. "That was my nephew's boat!"

The old man tried to rise, to reach the water, but his wound had weakened him too much. He collapsed back onto the sand, and this time he didn't get up.

Pryce reached him first, dropping to his knees beside the elderly villager. Doyle's breathing was labored, beneath the blood and sand.

"Had to save the goats," Doyle whispered. "Forty years I've tended this herd. Couldn't let those devils take them."

"Don't talk," Pryce said, pressing his hands against the wound to stem the bleeding. "We'll get you to the village, to Dr. Bennett—"

"No time for that, lad." Doyle's eyes found his. "Tell me we won. Tell me we sent them running."

Pryce looked toward the harbor, where the last Corsair ship was indeed retreating into the darkness. The seadrake had vanished as suddenly as it had appeared. But the cost . . .

"We won," he said simply.

Doyle nodded once, closed his eyes, and was still.

Kai knelt beside them. "Pryce, we need to move. The Corsairs are gone, but our forces are still scattered. And Thane—"

As if summoned by his name, the Dragonkin battlemaster appeared overhead, his dragon landing heavily nearby. Thane dismounted.

"Tragic," he said, surveying Doyle's body and the scattered remnants of the goat pen. "Such chaos could have been avoided with proper coordination."

"Proper coordination?" Pryce stood slowly, fists clenched. "You ordered the dragons to maintain elevation while the ships needed support!"

"I ordered tactical positioning to prevent friendly fire incidents," Thane replied smoothly. "Unfortunately, young leadership chose to abandon formation, creating the very confusion I sought to avoid."

"You knew those Corsairs were coming for the beach. You left us without support deliberately!"

Thane's expression remained infuriatingly calm. "I followed established protocols. It's hardly my fault if inexperienced commanders can't adapt to fluid battlefield conditions."

Other defenders were arriving now— Dragonkin and Shorling alike. Pryce could see them watching, listening, forming opinions about what had happened and who was to blame.

"Look at the results of your 'adaptation,'" Thane continued, gesturing toward the burning wreckage in the harbor. "One Shorling vessel lost.

Multiple injuries. An elderly civilian dead. All because proper chain of command was ignored."

"That's enough." Princess Seren appeared at the edge of the group, her dragon landing near them. "The battle is over. We should focus on casualties and damage assessment."

"Of course, Your Highness," Thane said with a perfect bow. "Though future engagements might benefit from clearer command structure. Perhaps battle-tested leadership rather than . . ." He let his gaze drift to Pryce, the implication clear.

Councilor Markham pushed through the crowd, his face flushed with exertion and anger. "What happened here? Why were our forces scattered when the attack came?"

"Equipment failure compromised communications," Thane explained before Pryce could speak. "Orders were misheard, formations broken. In the confusion, proper support couldn't be provided where needed."

"Equipment failure?" Kai said, indignation clear in his voice. "The equipment was fine until—"

"Until battlefield conditions overwhelmed undertrained operators," Thane finished. "Perhaps Crystal Shores would benefit from Dragonkin communications specialists. To prevent future misunderstandings."

Pryce watched in growing horror as Thane's narrative took hold. Around them, villagers nodded. The evidence supported his version—

scattered forces, confused orders, a dead elder and sunken fishing boat.

"This alliance was supposed to protect us," Markham said, his mustache bristling with fury. "Instead, our own allies nearly killed us!"

"The alliance remains strong," Seren said. "These were combat conditions. Confusion is inevitable."

"Inevitable?" A fisherman spat on the ground. "Tell that to the families whose boys went down with the Merry Catch. Tell that to Old Man Doyle!"

"Perhaps," Thane said, "this incident demonstrates the need for unified command. Crystal Shores has shown great courage, but courage alone cannot replace experience in complex military operations."

The implication was apparent: remove Pryce from command, place everything under Dragonkin authority, and such disasters wouldn't happen again.

Stormwing limped closer to Pryce, her injured wing dragging slightly in the sand. She pressed her great head against his shoulder.

"I need to tend to my dragon," Pryce said quietly. "And see to the wounded."

He turned away from the crowd, Kai falling into step beside him. Behind them, Thane's voice continued to weave its poisonous words, turning tonight's chaos into tomorrow's political opportunity.

"They're going to blame you for all of it," Kai said as they walked toward the village.

"Because I am to blame. I should have seen what Thane was doing."

"You saved lives tonight."

"But Shorlings died." Pryce looked back toward the harbor, where wreckage still smoldered. "Thane's right about one thing—I'm not experienced enough for this. People are dying because of my mistakes."

"People are dying because of Thane's sabotage," Kai corrected. "Don't let him twist this into something it's not."

But as they reached the village, Pryce could already see the doubt in people's faces. The alliance had held, barely, but its foundation had cracked. And tomorrow, Thane would be ready to exploit every fissure.

The war for Crystal Shores' future had claimed its first blood.

CHAPTER 12

The next morning, Crystal Shores was silent except for the sound of oars cutting through water. Six boats moved in slow procession toward the charred remnants of the Merry Catch, which had been towed closer to shore during the night.

Pryce stood at the edge of the pier, dark circles under his eyes from lack of sleep. Beside him, Kai slouched against a wooden piling. Neither had slept since the battle.

"Four bodies recovered so far," Harbormaster Westley said, approaching them. "Still searching for young Collins and old Reever."

Pryce nodded, his throat too tight for words. Each time the recovery boats returned with another shrouded form, a fresh wound opened in his heart. These were people he'd known his entire life—fishermen he'd learned from, neighbors who'd watched him grow up.

"They're saying—" Westley began, then stopped himself.

"They're saying what?" Kai asked, straightening.

The harbormaster's mouth tightened beneath his salt-and-pepper beard. "Nothing of consequence. Just tavern talk."

Pryce knew better. "They're saying it's my fault. That if I'd coordinated better with the Dragonkin forces, the Merry Catch wouldn't have been caught in the crossfire."

Westley didn't deny it. Instead, he shifted his weight and looked out at the recovery effort. "People need someone to blame when tragedy strikes. Battle is confusing. Mistakes happen."

"This wasn't a mistake," Kai said. "The Dragonkin warriors were deliberately positioned to create a crossfire situation."

"Careful with accusations like that," Westley warned. "Thane has the Queen's ear now."

As if summoned by his name, Thane appeared at the far end of the dock. Two Dragonkin guards flanked him as he walked toward them.

"Harper-Green," Thane called. "I came to offer the Dragonkin delegation's formal condolences for last night's losses."

Pryce forced himself to relax. "Thank you, Battlemaster."

Thane stopped before them, his posture perfect. "Such a tragedy might have been avoided with more experienced command," he said, loud enough to be heard by nearby villagers. "Perhaps in future engagements, my tactical expertise might benefit your defense coordination."

Kai shifted beside Pryce, a subtle movement that brought him half a step closer to Thane. His hand rested near the knife at his belt.

"The Queen has suggested I oversee all future defense operations," Thane continued, his gaze fixed on Pryce. "For the *safety* of Crystal Shores, of course."

A commotion from the recovery boats interrupted the conversation. The smallest boat was returning to shore, bearing another shrouded form.

"Young Collins," someone said as the craft docked. "Found tangled in the rigging."

Pryce turned away from Thane, moving toward the boat. Collins had been barely sixteen, eager to prove himself on his uncle's fishing crew. Pryce swallowed hard, remembering Doyle's death on the beach the night before—how the old man had died in his arms after trying to protect his beloved goats from the Corsair raiders. The image was still raw in his mind: Doyle's words "Tell me we won" his final request.

Both deaths—Collins at sea, Doyle on the shore—felt emblematic of Crystal Shores itself: stubborn, loyal to a fault, vulnerable.

"Such waste," Thane said, having followed Pryce to the boat's edge. "Boys dying on fishing boats when they could have been properly trained warriors—how very Shorling."

The contempt wrapped in false admiration was the final straw. Pryce whirled to face him. "Collins died serving his village. Doyle died protecting what he loved. That's something worth respecting, regardless of what it was."

Thane's eyes narrowed slightly, the only indication that Pryce's words had struck a nerve. "Of course," he said smoothly. "I meant no disrespect to your . . . quaint values."

Villagers had gathered now, forming a loose circle around the young body as it was carried from the boat. Faces streaked with grief and exhaustion turned toward the exchange between Pryce and Thane.

"The burial service will be at midday," Councilor Markham announced, stepping forward with authority. "All six of our fallen will be honored together."

"The Dragonkin delegation will attend," Thane said, with a slight bow. "To show our solidarity in these difficult times."

As he turned to leave, his sleeve brushed against a pile of recovered debris from the Merry Catch. Kai, whose attention had been fixed on the charred wood since it was brought ashore, suddenly frowned.

"Wait," he said, kneeling beside a blackened spar of wood. "Harbormaster, look at this burn pattern."

Westley crouched beside him, examining where Kai pointed. "Unusual," he said, running a finger along the scorch marks. "Not like any Corsair weapon I've seen."

Thane's expression shifted for an instant before settling back into neutrality. "Combat debris often shows strange damage patterns," he said dismissively. "Heat, water, impact—they create misleading effects."

But Westley was shaking his head. "Fifteen years as harbormaster, and I've never seen Corsair weapons leave burns like these." He looked up at Thane. "These look more like—"

"We should let the recovery teams continue their solemn work," Thane interrupted. "Battlemaster duties call me elsewhere. Harper-Green, my condolences again for your losses."

As Thane departed with his guards, Pryce noticed a small, folded paper near his boot. Faye stood at the edge of the gathered crowd. She met his eyes briefly, then glanced meaningfully at the paper before turning away.

Pryce casually retrieved it, palming the note as he stepped back from the crowd.

"We need to talk," Kai whispered. "Something's not right about those burn patterns."

"I know," Pryce said, discreetly opening Faye's note. *"Urgent evidence gathered. Meet at message center when you can slip away. Bring Kai."*

The message center was unusually quiet when Pryce and Kai arrived an hour later. Normally, Faye's trained gulls would be coming and going in a constant stream of activity, but today the birds sat quietly in their perches, as if respecting the village's grief.

"You're here," Faye said, looking up from her desk where papers were spread. "Close the door."

Pryce secured the latch. "What's so urgent?"

"These." She gestured to the documents before her. "The letters Pipwhistle stole from Thane. I've been analyzing them all morning, and . . ." She shook her head. "It's worse than we thought."

Kai leaned over the desk. "Correspondence with Corsair captains?"

"Not just correspondence. Coordination." Faye picked up one letter. "This one details Crystal Shores' defense weaknesses—harbor approach vectors, patrol schedules, even the load capacity of our dock pilings."

"Strategic intelligence," Pryce said, feeling ill. "He's been feeding them information about exactly where to strike."

"That's just the beginning." Faye arranged several pages in sequence. "These messages reference 'extraction points' and 'resource locations' that have nothing to do with typical invasion plans."

Kai frowned. "What kind of resources would Corsairs want from Crystal Shores? We're a fishing village with some timber supplies at best."

"That's what confused me at first," Faye said. "Until I remembered something Thane said when he first arrived—that casual comment about Crystal Shores having 'hidden value' beneath the surface."

A soft rustling sound near the window made them all turn. Pipwhistle stood there. Neither Pryce nor Kai had heard him enter.

"The Quibnocket sees what others miss," Pipwhistle said. "And what I see beneath your feet would make dragons weep with greed."

He approached the desk, producing a rolled parchment from within his cloak. When he unfurled it across Faye's desk, they saw an intricate map of Crystal Shores and its surrounding area—but unlike any map they'd seen before. This one showed layers beneath the village, with strange glowing veins marked in metallic ink and annotated with Dragonkin runes.

"Where did you get this?" Pryce asked, studying the elaborate document.

"From the Queen's own tent," Pipwhistle said. "Her guards possess sharp eyes but dull minds. They watch for shadows while I dance in plain sight."

Kai traced the strange markings. "These symbols . . . I don't recognize them."

"We need Finnegan," Pryce said. "He spent years studying Dragonkin texts."

Faye nodded. "He should be finished preparing Doyle for burial."

***

Old Man Finnegan's cottage sat at the edge of the lake, its walls leaning slightly inland as if perpetually bracing against a storm. When they arrived, he was washing his hands in a basin.

"Forgive the mess," he said, gesturing vaguely around the cluttered main room. "Didn't expect company on a burial day."

His eyes fell on the map Pryce spread across his table. His entire demeanor changed in an instant.

"Where did you get this?" His voice had dropped to a whisper. He reached for his walking stick, using it to swiftly secure the door bolt.

"Pipwhistle . . . found it," Pryce said, watching the old man's reaction.

Finnegan moved toward a bookshelf, pulling specific volumes and carvings to reveal a hidden panel in the wall. "Into the back room. All of you. Now."

They followed him into a concealed chamber lit by a single window high in the wall. Shelves lined with books, scrolls, and strange artifacts covered every available surface. At the center stood a worn table.

"This map shouldn't exist," Finnegan said, carefully spreading the parchment on the table. "The Binding ensured these records were destroyed centuries ago."

"The Binding?" Kai asked.

Finnegan pointed at the glowing veins on the map. "Dragon magic ore," he said. "The rarest, most valuable resource in all the known waters. And this map shows Crystal Shores sitting atop the richest deposit ever discovered."

Pryce leaned closer, memories flooding back—the hidden war chamber on Dragon's Fang Island, the maps and surveys he'd discovered with Kestrel's notes marked in red ink. *Primary ore deposits here. Deep mining required. Estimated yield: enough dragon-magic ore to arm three battalions.*

"This is why they want Crystal Shores," Pryce said. "I should have known they wouldn't give up so easily. The dragon-magic ore beneath our village is too valuable to them." He placed both hands on the table, leaning forward as he studied the details. "Seren told me it was the largest deposit they'd ever discovered. Their entire invasion—the fake Seadrake Corsair threat, my transformation, even that mockery of a wedding ceremony over my supposedly dead body—it was all to establish a legal claim to these minerals."

Finnegan jabbed a finger at the marked deposits. "Wars have been fought over deposits a tenth this size."

Faye frowned, thumbing through the letters she had brought. "If it's so valuable, why hasn't it been mined already?"

"Because extraction nearly destroyed us all once before," Finnegan said. He reached for an ancient, leather-bound book, its pages yellow with age. "Three hundred years ago, the first Shorling settlements here weren't fishing villages at all. They were mining camps."

He opened the book to reveal illustrations of early settlers using strange devices to extract glowing material from lakeside caverns.

"The mining attracted both Dragonkin and Corsairs. A three-way conflict erupted, but the real disaster came when the mining disturbed ancient dragon nesting sites deep beneath the lake."

"Nightfathom," Pryce whispered, remembering the legends.

Finnegan nodded. "And others like him. Primordial lake dragons who'd slumbered for millennia. Their awakening nearly destroyed all three populations until The Binding was created."

"What exactly was The Binding?" Pryce asked.

"A magical treaty. Representatives from Shorlings, dragons, and Dragonkin contributed blood to a ritual that sealed the deepest ore deposits and established boundaries for coexistence." Finnegan's eyes drifted to the faint scales on Pryce's jawline. "Blood from certain families—including yours, Pryce."

"The Binding prevented massive extraction," Finnegan continued. "Small-scale surface mining was permitted, but the main deposits were sealed with magic that requires all three bloodlines to unlock. Breaking that seal without the proper ritual would risk catastrophic consequences."

A shuffling sound made them all turn. There, perched atop a bookshelf that had been empty seconds before, sat Pipwhistle. Between his fingers, he twirled what appeared to be a blueprint.

"Great depths!" Finnegan exclaimed, nearly falling over. "One of these days you're going to give an old sailor a heart attack, you mischievous sprite. Is it too much to ask for a proper door entrance like civilized folk?"

Pipwhistle's grin widened, showing teeth that needed brushing. "Doors, windows, chimneys—all such tedious paths, when space itself has so many interesting wrinkles to slip through." He tossed the blueprint onto the table where it unfurled, revealing complex schematics of a massive drilling apparatus. "This little treasure was gathering dust in the Queen's private collection."

"Mining equipment," Kai said, recognizing the basic framework. "But it looks more advanced than anything I've seen before."

"Because it combines Corsair technology with Dragonkin magic," Finnegan explained. "Neither group could extract the ore alone. Corsairs lack the magical affinity to work with dragon-infused materials, while Dragonkin lack the mechanical expertise for deep extraction."

"So they've formed an alliance," Pryce said, the full picture becoming horrifyingly clear. "The Corsair attacks, Nymeria's offer of protection, the betrothal—it was all a scheme to gain control of Crystal Shores and the ore beneath it."

Faye was examining another of Thane's letters. "According to this timeline, they planned to let the Corsairs damage Crystal Shores enough to justify Dragonkin occupation, then divide the mining rights between them."

"Last night's attack," Kai said. "That wasn't just a test of our defenses—"

"They planned to pick off our defenses one by one," Pryce finished. "The friendly fire incidents, the confusion in the command chain—Thane orchestrated it all to weaken us for the main assault."

Finnegan traced the mining locations on the map. "According to these charts, they'd start extraction directly beneath the village square. Our homes would be hollowed out within weeks."

"And if they break The Binding?" Faye asked quietly.

Finnegan's expression darkened. "The ancient texts suggest it wasn't just a treaty but a magical necessity. Breaking it risks releasing the lake guardians and triggering geological instability throughout the region."

"So they're not just threatening Crystal Shores," Pryce said, "but potentially the entire lake ecosystem."

"For dragon magic ore?" Kai shook his head in disbelief. "Is it really worth that risk?"

"Dragon magic ore isn't just valuable—it's power in its purest form," Finnegan said. "With enough of it, Nymeria could forge weapons capable of conquering every settlement around Lake Dragontide. And the Corsairs could create magical devices beyond our understanding."

Pryce stared at the evidence spread before them. "We need to warn the village. Show them what's really happening."

"And who would believe us?" Kai asked. "Half the village already blames you for last night's deaths. They're more likely to listen to Thane."

"Then we need more than just these documents," Pryce said. "We need witnesses. People who've seen Thane's coordination with the Corsairs firsthand."

Faye sorted through the remaining papers. "There's mention here of a final coordination meeting before the main attack. Thane plans to use light signals from the lighthouse tonight to confirm attack positions."

"When water runs red and sky burns black, look not to the horizon but beneath your feet for the true enemy," Pipwhistle said, then produced one final document—a Corsair captain's log confirming payment arrangements for ore extraction rights.

"So what do we do?" Kai asked, looking to Pryce. "We can't go to Mayor Wright—not with Thane having her ear. And half the council already thinks you're incompetent."

Pryce straightened, a plan forming in his mind. "We don't need the whole council. Just enough witnesses to expose Thane's treachery before the main Corsair fleet arrives." He turned to Faye. "Can your birds carry messages to the lookout posts without being intercepted?"

"Of course," she replied, already understanding his direction.

"Good. We'll need Jorr from Emberfall too—if anyone can speak to Dragonkin deserters, it's him."

"What about Princess Seren?" Finnegan asked. "Is she involved in this conspiracy?"

Pryce hesitated. "I don't know. But we need to find out before we make our move."

"And when exactly are we making this move?" Kai asked.

Pryce looked at each of them in turn. "Tonight. When Thane goes to signal the Corsairs, we'll be waiting. With witnesses."

Outside, the wind picked up, rattling the cottage's shutters. Beneath their feet lay untold wealth and power. Above them, in just a few hours, the funeral bells would toll for Old Man Doyle and the other victims of a battle that was merely the opening move in a more dangerous game.

"When dragons hunt with sharks," Pipwhistle said, "small fish should swim very deep or very far."

"We're not swimming away," Pryce said.

As if in response, a distant rumble of thunder rolled across the lake—either a warning, or a promise.

CHAPTER 13

Crystal Shores' cemetery occupied a gentle slope overlooking the lake, its stones bearing the names of generations who had lived and died by Dragontide's waters. Today, six fresh graves marked the earth, the soil still dark beneath a sky that wept a gentle, persistent rain.

Pryce stood among the gathered villagers, the cool droplets mingling with tears on many faces. His formal clothes felt too tight across his shoulders. Beside the open graves, the shrouded bodies waited for their final rest.

Mayor Wright stepped forward, her ceremonial blue sash darkened by rain. "We gather today to return our fallen to the embrace of Lake Dragontide," she began, her voice carrying across the hushed crowd. "Old Man Doyle, whose goats have kept us in milk and cheese for many years. Young Collins, who had just begun to learn the ways of the deep waters. Harbormaster Jensen, whose knowledge of tides kept our ships safe."

As she named each of the fallen, family members stepped forward to place a personal token in their loved one's grave—a fishing lure, a carved wooden goat, a carefully preserved chart. Shorling tradition held that these items would guide the departed back to the lake in their next life.

Through the crowd, Pryce caught glimpses of Dragonkin scales. Thane and his delegation stood slightly apart. Queen Nymeria had not attended, but Princess Seren stood at the forefront of the Dragonkin mourners, her eyes meeting Pryce's briefly across the distance.

"Shorlings know the lake gives, and the lake takes," Mayor Wright continued. "We do not rage against its tides, but honor those who have returned to its depths."

Pryce felt a subtle nudge against his ribs. Kai had positioned himself nearby, he whispered from the corner of his mouth. "Westley confirmed it. The burn patterns on the Merry Catch—they match Dragonkin weapons, not Corsair."

Pryce gave the slightest nod, keeping his eyes on the ceremony. The evidence mounting against Thane would mean nothing without witnesses— and for that, they needed time.

Old Man Doyle's daughter stepped forward, casting a handful of soil into her father's grave. "He died protecting what he loved," she said, voice breaking. "His precious goats, his piece of shoreline.

Simple things, perhaps, but they were his to protect."

From the Dragonkin delegation, Pryce noticed Thane leaning to whisper something to a scaled guard. The guard nodded almost imperceptibly before slipping away through the crowd.

"Tonight," Kai whispered, following Pryce's gaze. "Lighthouse point. Finnegan says that's where they've been sending signals."

The ceremony continued, each family sharing memories of the fallen as tradition demanded. When Doyle's granddaughter spoke of his stubborn refusal to leave his animals during the attack, many villagers nodded in understanding. Shorling life was built on such determination—the kind that seemed foolish until it became the difference between survival and death.

As the final prayers were spoken, mourners began the slow procession back to the village. The rain softened to a misty drizzle. Ahead, Thane walked, occasionally inclining his head to accept condolences from villagers seeking to curry favor with the Dragonkin delegation.

"He's planning something tonight," Pryce said to Kai. "I can feel it."

Kai nodded. "Faye's messengers are already in position. And Jorr should be back by now."

As they crested the hill leading down to Crystal Shores, Pryce looked back at the freshly filled graves. Six mounds of earth that might have been avoided if not for Thane's deliberate interference with their defenses. Six lives sacrificed not to Corsair raids but to Dragonkin ambition.

"We'll make it right," Pryce said softly. "Tonight."

***

Finnegan's cottage had become their impromptu headquarters. By dusk, the main room buzzed with quiet but intense activity as final preparations were made.

Faye sat cross-legged on the floor, carefully attaching tiny message capsules to the legs of her Tidewing gulls. The birds waited with patience, as if sensing the gravity of their mission.

"Northwest lookout confirmed," she reported, releasing one bird through the window. "That's all our observation points covered. Each has instructions to document whatever they see."

Pryce nodded, studying the rough map of the lighthouse point spread across Finnegan's table. "How much longer until—"

A soft knock at the door silenced everyone. Kai moved swiftly to a position beside the entrance, spear held ready, while Finnegan shuffled forward.

"Who sails in fog?" the old man called—their arranged challenge.

"Those who trust their ears above their eyes," came the reply in Jorr's voice.

Finnegan unbolted the door, opening it just wide enough for a quick assessment before swinging it fully open. Jorr ducked inside, followed by three hooded figures who kept their faces carefully hidden.

"You found them," Pryce said.

"It wasn't easy. Trust is in short supply these days." Jorr gestured to his companions, who slowly lowered their hoods.

The first was a young woman with short dark hair and copper-tinged scales visible at her temples. Pryce's eyes widened in recognition.

"This is Raven," Jorr said. "She was a trainee rider at Dragon's Fang Island."

"We've met," Pryce said, nodding to her. "During my training days."

Raven returned his nod with a faint smile. "Harper-Green. Your Stormwing has grown since those early lessons."

"You two know each other?" Kai asked, looking between them.

Jorr grinned. "Raven helped teach Pryce some basic maneuvers when he first arrived at Dragon's Fang. She was one of the few who showed him kindness when most others . . ." He let the sentence trail off.

"She rode that copper drake," Pryce added, memories flooding back. "Made flying look effortless while I was still struggling to stay in the saddle."

"You learned quickly enough. And now we both find ourselves on unexpected paths," Raven said. "I overheard Thane discussing coordinated attack patterns with someone using a Corsair signaling device. When I questioned it, I was reassigned to mucking out dragon pens."

The second figure was barely more than a boy, his copper-colored scales more prominent than most half-bloods.

"Aurix," Jorr introduced him. "He served as messenger between ships."

"Third-year apprentice to Master Kestrel, if I remember correctly," Pryce said with a look of recognition. "You escorted me around Drakemere when I first arrived."

Aurix bowed his head slightly. "You have a good memory, Harper-Green. I didn't think you'd recall a mere attendant among so many faces."

"Hard to forget someone who saved me from walking into the wrong chamber during that first formal dinner." Pryce smiled. "I nearly blundered into Queen Nymeria's private quarters instead of the great hall."

"The queen would not have been pleased," Aurix said.

"You were always quick with directions," Pryce said. "Made you perfect for your messenger duties between the ships."

"Until I began delivering messages I wasn't meant to see," Aurix said. "I carried orders that didn't match what the commanders told their troops. Double messages—one set for official channels, another for Thane's inner circle."

The third figure was older, his scales a deep iron gray that matched his close-cropped hair. "This is my cousin, Ironhide," Jorr said. "He served in the Queen's guard."

"Until I heard too much," Ironhide said. "Nymeria and Thane discussing extraction schedules, the composition of the lake bed beneath Crystal Shores. Mining plans, not defense strategies."

"You all understand the risk you're taking?" Pryce asked. "Testifying against a battlemaster—"

"We understand honor," Raven interrupted. "Something Thane knows nothing about. Dragons mate for life, fight for their territory openly. They don't slither in shadows, making deals with sworn enemies."

Kai had been quietly assessing the three deserters. "You really believe they'll listen to you? Over Thane?"

"They'll listen to evidence," Ironhide replied. "Dragonkin respect strength, but we despise treachery. If Thane has indeed allied with Corsairs— ancient enemies who hunt dragons for sport—many warriors will turn against him."

"These might help," Finnegan said, retrieving a wooden case from his back room. He opened it to reveal a collection of crystal lenses mounted in brass housings. "Magnification devices. They'll allow your witnesses to see the lighthouse signals clearly, even from a distance."

Faye released another bird, then turned to the group. "All observers report clear skies now. Stars visible. Perfect conditions for signal lights."

"What about Emberstriker?" Pryce asked Jorr. "Has she recovered?"

A small smile crossed Jorr's face. "She's doing well. Tempest has hardly left her side—treats her like a hatchling sibling." His expression grew serious again. "But these three weren't my only discovery. There are rumors of Corsair ships massing beyond Stormshroud Isles. The main fleet could arrive within days."

"Then tonight is our only chance," Pryce said. "If we can expose Thane's treachery before the fleet arrives—"

A familiar tinkling laugh interrupted him. Everyone turned to find Pipwhistle sitting atop Finnegan's bookshelf, legs dangling as he polished what appeared to be a brass object.

"By the deep, man!" Finnegan exclaimed. "Must you always appear like some ghost from the lake's bottom?"

"Ghosts walk through walls," Pipwhistle replied with a grin. "I simply step sideways when no one's looking." He tossed the brass object to Pryce, who caught it reflexively.

It was a captain's seal—the kind used to mark official Corsair communications.

"Where did you get this?" Pryce asked, examining the intricate insignia.

"From a pocket that wasn't mine," Pipwhistle said cheerfully. "Attached to a log that wasn't mine, documenting payments that certainly weren't mine." He produced a leather-bound journal from within his patchwork cloak. "Captain's log of the Corsair vessel *Blackwater*. Full of fascinating entries about 'mineral rights' and 'coordinated extractions' and 'the battlemaster's guarantee of Shorling compliance.'"

Kai whistled softly. "That's . . . actual proof."

"Proof is like fish," Pipwhistle said, his expression turning suddenly serious. "Doesn't stay fresh long. Best used quickly."

Pryce examined the journal. "With this, and witnesses to Thane's signals tonight, we might convince enough of the council to take action."

Finnegan unrolled a detailed map of the lighthouse point across the table. "You can't just confront him openly. He'll deny everything, and his guards will protect him. You need to document him in the act, catch him sending signals to Corsair scouts."

"Which means we need to position ourselves carefully," Pryce said, studying the map. "Raven, Aurix, and Ironhide should be placed where they can clearly see the signals but remain hidden from Thane's guards."

Kai pointed to three ridges overlooking the lighthouse. "Here, here, and here. Good visibility, decent cover. I'll take the south approach with Finnegan's magnification lenses."

"Faye's birds can deliver confirmation messages between positions," Jorr added.

As they worked out the final details of their plan, a strange stillness fell over the cottage. Outside, the last light faded from the sky, revieling stars untouched by clouds. Perfect weather for signal lights to carry across the water.

"What if we're wrong?" Faye asked. "What if he's just . . . conducting legitimate patrols?"

"We're not wrong," Pryce said, touching the Quibnocket token in his pocket. "Too many pieces fit together now. The sabotaged training, the contradictory orders during battle, the letters to neighboring villages . . . Thane has been systematically isolating Crystal Shores to make us dependent on Dragonkin 'protection.'"

"And the princess?" Jorr asked quietly. "Where does she stand in all this?"

Pryce hesitated. "I don't know. But I hope—"

A sharp knock at the door froze everyone mid-sentence. This time, no challenge had been arranged, no visitors expected. Kai moved silently to his position beside the entrance, while Jorr herded the Dragonkin deserters toward the back room.

Finnegan grabbed his walking stick, approaching the door cautiously. "Who's there?" he called, his voice deliberately gruff.

"Someone who needs answers," came a woman's voice. "Open the door."

Pryce recognized that voice immediately. He met Finnegan's questioning gaze and nodded.

When the door swung open, Princess Seren stood alone on the threshold. Her eyes surveyed the room, taking in the maps, the evidence, the preparations.

"So," she said quietly, "you know."

"About the ore deposits? About Thane's coordination with the Corsairs?" Pryce asked. "Yes. We know."

Seren stepped inside, closing the door behind her. "My mother sent me to find you. She says you've been acting suspiciously, gathering potential dissidents." Her eyes found the Dragonkin deserters partially hidden in the back room. "She wasn't wrong."

Tension crackled through the cottage. Kai's grip tightened on his spear.

"Are you here to stop us?" Pryce asked.

Seren was silent for a long moment, her gaze moving from face to face before settling on Pryce. "I'm here because I need to know if you have proof. Real proof, not just suspicions."

Wordlessly, Pryce held out Pipwhistle's stolen journal. Seren took it, flipping through the pages with increasing intensity.

"Where did you get this?" she demanded.

"Does it matter?" Pryce countered. "Is it authentic?"

Her eyes lifted from the page. "This is Captain Redblade's seal. He's one of the most notorious Corsair leaders in the eastern waters." She closed the journal. "And yes, it appears authentic."

"Then you know what Thane is planning. What your mother authorized."

"I know what I've been told. That Crystal Shores sits atop resources vital to Dragonkin security. That an alliance would benefit both our peoples."

"And the deaths?" Kai asked sharply. "The sabotage? Was that for 'both our peoples' too?"

"I didn't know," Seren said. "I didn't want to know. But after last night's battle, after seeing Thane deliberately position our forces to create a crossfire situation . . ." She sighed. "Tonight, he plans to signal the main Corsair fleet. The coordinates for their final assault."

"How do you know this?" Jorr asked.

"Because I was ordered to stay away from the lighthouse. All Dragonkin were—except Thane's inner circle." She looked directly at Pryce. "If you're going to expose him, it needs to be tonight. With witnesses that both Shorlings and Dragonkin will believe."

Pryce studied her face, searching for deception. "Why help us? He serves your mother."

"He serves himself," Seren replied. "And my mother has forgotten what it means to be worthy of a dragon's bond. I made a mistake last time, at Dragon's Fang Island. I won't make it again."

Outside, the moon had risen, casting silver light across Crystal Shores. From the harbor came the faint sounds of watch changes, of patrols setting out for their nighttime positions.

"We need to move," Finnegan said, checking the position of the stars visible through his small window. "Thane will signal at high tide—less than an hour from now."

Pryce looked at each person in the cottage— Kai with his spear and unwavering loyalty; Faye with her messenger birds; Jorr and his Dragonkin allies risking everything for principle; Pipwhistle with his impossible abilities; Finnegan with his knowledge of ancient conflicts; and Seren, making a choice that could cost her everything.

"Tonight," Pryce said. "When Thane goes to signal the Corsairs, we'll be waiting. With witnesses."

CHAPTER 14

Night blanketed Lighthouse Point, the stars scattered across the sky like salt across a fisherman's table. Pryce crouched behind a cluster of rocks, his eyes fixed on the lighthouse tower. Beside him, Kai adjusted the focus of his spyglass.

"Any movement?" Pryce whispered.

"Nothing yet." Kai lowered the spyglass. "But it's still early. Finnegan said the lighthouse keeper wouldn't be relieved until third bell."

The vantage point they'd chosen gave them a clear view of both the lighthouse and the lake beyond. Dark water stretched to the horizon. Somewhere out there, Corsair ships waited.

Behind them, concealed in the shadows of stunted pine trees, Princess Seren stood with Jorr and the Dragonkin deserters.

Pryce moved away from Kai, making his way to where Seren stood apart from the others.

"You don't have to be here," he said quietly. "If Thane is caught signaling the Corsairs—"

"If he's caught betraying Crystal Shores, he betrays the Dragonkin as well," Seren interrupted. "Though I suspect my mother won't see it that way."

"This could put you in an impossible position."

"I've been in an impossible position since I arrived in Crystal Shores." She glanced toward the lighthouse. "But tonight, at least, I choose where I stand."

"Even if it means standing against your mother?"

"Let's hope it doesn't come to that."

"Movement," Kai called softly. "Approaching from the eastern path."

Pryce hurried back to his position. Through the spyglass, he could make out three figures climbing the winding path toward the lighthouse: Thane and two Dragonkin guards.

"It's him," Pryce confirmed. "And he's not alone."

"More guards means more witnesses," Jorr said as he joined them. "Better for us."

Raven and Aurix crept forward, taking positions where they could clearly observe the lighthouse entrance. Aurix had brought writing materials to document what they witnessed.

"Remember," Pryce said to the group, "we need convincing proof. No one moves until Thane actually sends signals and we receive confirmation from Pipwhistle."

"Where is that patchwork trickster, anyway?" Kai said, scanning the area. "He should have been here by now."

"Pipwhistle appears when needed, not when expected," Pryce said, remembering his mother's stories.

They watched as Thane reached the lighthouse door. Words were exchanged with the keeper—too distant to hear, but the body language suggested authority being exercised. Moments later, the keeper descended the path alone, heading back toward the village.

"He's dismissed the regular keeper," Kai whispered. "Taking control himself."

Time stretched like pulled taffy as they watched Thane enter the lighthouse. Minutes later, the beacon light at the top began to move in a deliberate pattern—three long sweeps toward the west, followed by two short flashes.

"He's starting," Pryce said. "But what do the signals mean?"

"They mean treachery wears silver scales tonight." Pipwhistle appeared beside them so suddenly that Kai nearly tumbled backward in surprise. The Quibnocket grinned.

"Must you always do that?" Kai said, regaining his balance.

"The expected loses its savor." Pipwhistle produced a leather-bound book from within his motley garment. "Besides, acquiring this required . . . creative timing."

Kai stared at the Quibnocket, eyes narrowing suspiciously as he glanced at the voluminous cloak. "Do you just carry everything in there? First stolen letters, then maps, now a whole codebook? Is there a small village hidden in the folds of that thing? Perhaps a library and tavern?"

Pipwhistle's eyes twinkled. "A cloak is but a door to possibilities, young Frostborne. Some find only cloth and thread. Others . . ." he patted the garment lovingly, producing a faint jingling of unseen objects, ". . . find whatever the moment requires."

"Remind me never to play hide-and-seek with you," Kai said, turning his attention back to the codebook.

Pryce took the book, recognizing it instantly as a Corsair naval codebook. Its leather cover was stained and worn, the corners reinforced with metal caps.

"Where did you get this?" he asked, even as he opened it to find pages of signal codes and their meanings.

"Let's just say a Corsair scout captain is currently searching his quarters for this very book," Pipwhistle replied with a mischievous gleam in his eye. "And will likely have his fingers removed for its loss."

Aurix moved closer. "That's a captain's personal codebook. How did you—"

"Questions dim the glory of achievement," Pipwhistle interrupted with a dismissive wave. "The signals—note them quickly."

Pryce turned to Aurix, who had his writing instruments ready. "Record the pattern: three long west, two short."

As they watched, Thane's signals continued—complex patterns of light sweeping across the lake in what had seemed random movements but now, with the codebook in hand, revealed themselves as deliberate messages.

"According to this," Pryce said, flipping through the codebook, "he's confirming attack coordinates." His finger traced the translation. "'Harbor approach clear. Defense positions as mapped. Proceed at dawn.'"

"He's telling them exactly where to strike," Raven said.

Kai raised his spyglass toward the distant horizon. "There—look!"

Far out on the lake, barely visible against the night, pinpricks of light flashed in response—three short bursts followed by one long.

"Confirmation received," Pryce translated from the codebook. "The Corsair fleet acknowledges his signal."

"We have him," Kai said. "Red-handed treason."

"We move now," Seren said. "Before he sends more detailed information."

They descended upon the lighthouse—Pryce, Kai, and Jorr from the front path; Raven and Aurix circling to cover the rear exit; Princess Seren walking openly up the main steps.

Thane was still manipulating the lighthouse beam when Seren pushed open the door, with Pryce and the others close behind her. From his position just behind the princess, Pryce watched the battlemaster turn, surprised.

"Princess Seren," Thane said, offering a bow that somehow managed to seem both respectful and dismissive. "What brings you to the lighthouse at this late hour?"

Pryce observed how Thane's posture changed—relaxing slightly at the sight of Seren alone, before tensing again as he spotted the others entering behind her.

"I might ask you the same, Battlemaster," Seren replied. "Particularly regarding your fascination with signal codes."

Thane's eyes narrowed. Pryce noticed the two guards behind Thane moving uncomfortably, their hands drifting toward their weapons. He readied himself to move if things escalated.

"Military communication, Your Highness. Standard practice for coordinating defenses."

"Is that what you call it?" Pryce asked, near Seren, the Corsair codebook open in his hands.

"Strange that your 'standard practice' aligns perfectly with Corsair attack coordination signals."

The momentary flash of alarm in Thane's eyes confirmed everything. It vanished quickly beneath his mask of arrogance.

"Harper-Green," he said with a cold smile. "Still playing at leadership, I see. These accusations are beneath response."

"Then perhaps this evidence deserves your attention," Jorr said, presenting the documents they had gathered—Thane's letters to Corsair captains, geological surveys of Crystal Shores with ore deposits marked, and Aurix's detailed notes of the signals just witnessed.

Thane's guards exchanged uncertain glances. One took a half-step away from Thane.

"This is absurd," Thane said, though a hint of desperation had crept into his voice. "These are obvious forgeries."

"Are they?" Seren asked. She turned to the guards. "You've just witnessed your battlemaster sending signals that match Corsair attack codes. Will you stand with a traitor against your princess?"

The guards' hesitation was all the answer needed.

"You overstep, Princess," Thane said, his hand moving to his dagger. "The Queen herself authorized—"

He stopped abruptly, but the damage was done.

"The Queen," Seren repeated. "My mother authorized coordination with Corsairs against Crystal Shores?"

"Military strategy is beyond your understanding," Thane said, abandoning pretense. His eyes swept the group. "You think you've won something here? You've merely accelerated the inevitable."

The guards had made their decision. They stepped away from Thane, turning to face him with weapons drawn.

"By the authority of Princess Seren," Kai declared, "you're relieved of duty and held for treason against both Crystal Shores and the honor of the Dragonkin realm."

Thane laughed. "You think this changes anything? The fleet is already in position. Dawn will still bring fire and death to your pathetic village."

As the guards moved to restrain him, Thane's posture shifted subtly. Pryce, recognizing the coiled tension of a fighter preparing to strike, lunged forward just as Thane made his move.

The battlemaster's elbow connected with one guard's throat. As the Dragonkin soldier dropped, Thane spun toward the second guard, dagger appearing in his hand as if conjured from air.

Kai intercepted the strike with the wooden shaft of his spear, forcing the blade away. Jorr tackled Thane from the side, his substantial weight driving both of them against the lighthouse wall.

For a moment, Thane seemed subdued—then his head snapped forward, connecting with Jorr's nose. As Jorr reeled back, Thane broke free, dagger flashing in the dim light.

"Enough!" Seren shouted. "Stand down, Battlemaster!"

Thane hesitated, caught between respect for royal authority and his own desperation. It was enough. Pryce and Kai seized him from behind, forcing his arms behind his back.

"This accomplishes nothing," Thane said as cold iron manacles—brought for this very purpose—closed around his wrists. "The wheels are already in motion. The Corsair fleet comes with the dawn, and with them, your doom."

"Then we'll face it without a traitor in our midst," Pryce said.

As they led Thane down from the lighthouse, Pipwhistle appeared on the path.

"The small victory flows into larger battles," the Quibnocket said. "The Queen's tent stirs with activity. Royal guards gather. The spider feels the web tremble."

"My mother knows," Seren said.

"Word travels faster than feet when betrayal is the message," Pipwhistle confirmed.

"Then we need to move quickly," Pryce said. "Raven, Aurix—take Thane to the village cells. Kai, gather the witnesses. We need to present this evidence to the council immediately."

"And if Queen Nymeria intervenes?" Kai asked.

Seren straightened. "Then she will find herself facing both her daughter and the truth. Neither will yield easily."

"Ring the warning bells!" Pryce commanded as they descended from the lighthouse, Thane in restraints between them. "Three long, three short—emergency council summons."

The village bells began to peal within minutes, their urgent clangor cutting through the night's stillness. Windows lit throughout Crystal Shores as villagers awakened to the alarm. Men and women spilled into streets, some holding weapons, others clutching children close.

"Make way!" Kai shouted as they pushed through the gathering crowd. "Council emergency!"

The Great Hall filled rapidly. Elders arrived in nightclothes hastily covered with coats. Lanterns blazed around the council table as Mayor Wright entered.

"The Corsair fleet approaches with first light," Pryce announced. "We have perhaps an hour before they reach our shores."

By the time the eastern sky began to pale with approaching dawn, Crystal Shores had split into factions. The council chamber hummed with frightened voices as Pryce laid out the evidence— Thane's betrayal, the Corsair codebook, the coordinated signals, and the ore deposits beneath Crystal Shores that had motivated it all.

Mayor Wright sat at the head of the emergency council, her face gray with exhaustion. Around the table, councilors and village elders talked among themselves.

"This is why they wanted our village," Pryce concluded. "Not for strategic position or diplomatic advantage, but for what lies beneath our feet— dragon magic ore. The most valuable resource in the known world."

"And Queen Nymeria knew?" Councilor Markham asked. "Authorized this betrayal?"

"Thane all but admitted it," Seren said, standing beside Pryce. "My mother didn't come to Crystal Shores for alliance. She came for conquest— using Corsairs as her opening gambit."

The council chamber doors burst open. Queen Nymeria swept in, flanked by Dragonkin royal guards. Her midnight blue cloak billowed around her, and her silver eyes flashed with cold fury.

"What is the meaning of this?" she demanded. "My battlemaster detained? My daughter conspiring with Shorlings against her own blood?"

"Mother," Seren said. "Battlemaster Thane has been caught in acts of treason against both Crystal Shores and the honor of Dragonkin. We have proof—"

"You have nothing!" Nymeria said. "Release him immediately, or face the consequences of defying your queen."

Mayor Wright rose. "With respect, Your Majesty, we have evidence of collaboration with enemies who have already killed Shorling villagers. We cannot—"

"Evidence?" Nymeria interrupted. "You have forged documents and the word of traitors and deserters. This council has no authority over Dragonkin military operations."

"Military operations that involve sacrificing Crystal Shores to Corsair raiders?" Pryce challenged. "We caught Thane signaling the Corsair fleet. We translated his messages with their own codebook. Dawn brings their attack—precisely as he coordinated it."

The chamber erupted in panicked voices. Through the windows, the first pink streaks of sunrise painted the eastern sky. Time was running out.

Nymeria's gaze swept the room. "Very well. If Corsairs approach, we shall defend Crystal Shores— as allies. But proper command must be established. Battlemaster Thane will oversee—"

"No." Pryce said. "Thane has betrayed both our peoples. He will remain detained until this crisis passes."

"You dare—" Nymeria began, but the room suddenly fell silent as a distant boom shook the council chamber windows.

"Cannon fire," Harbormaster Westley said from the doorway. "The Corsair fleet is here. At least a dozen ships approaching from the west."

"Just as Thane signaled them," Kai added.

Crystal Shores fractured along invisible lines. Some Dragonkin guards moved to stand with Nymeria, while others—including Raven and Aurix—remained near Pryce and Seren. Villagers similarly divided, uncertain who to trust in this moment of crisis.

"We don't have time for division," Pryce said, addressing everyone. "The Corsairs are coming. Whatever differences exist between us must wait. Mayor Wright, Harbormaster Westley—activate all defense protocols. Kai, organize the volunteer brigades."

"And who will command our Dragonkin forces?" Nymeria asked. "You, perhaps? A boy playing at leadership?"

"I will," Seren said, stepping away from Pryce to face her mother directly. "As royal princess, in protection of our honor."

Mother and daughter locked gazes in silent battle. Finally, Nymeria inclined her head slightly— not agreement, but temporary ceasefire.

"Very well, daughter. Show me your . . . leadership." The way she emphasized the final word made it clear she expected failure.

Another boom shook the building, closer this time. Smoke began to rise from the western harbor.

"To your positions!" Mayor Wright commanded. "All civilians to the shelters! Every able defender to their stations!"

As the council chamber emptied, Pryce found himself momentarily alone with Seren and Nymeria.

"This changes nothing," Nymeria said, her voice pitched for their ears alone. "When this battle ends, there will be a reckoning."

"Yes," Seren replied, meeting her mother's gaze. "There will be."

Nymeria swept from the room, royal guards in formation around her.

"Can we trust her?" Pryce asked.

"To fight Corsairs? Yes. My mother despises them as much as she covets what lies beneath Crystal Shores. But after the battle? Trust nothing."

They emerged from the council hall into chaos. Smoke billowed from the harbor, where the first Corsair projectiles had struck the outer docks. Villagers ran in all directions—some toward shelters, others toward defense positions. Through it all, conflicting orders created confusion as Dragonkin and Shorling commanders struggled to coordinate.

At the harbor's edge, Thane's guards had arrived with the detained battlemaster. Queen Nymeria stood with them, clearly intending to release him.

"This is madness," Kai said, appearing at Pryce's side. "They're going to free him while Corsairs are literally bombarding the harbor."

"Not if I can help it," Pryce replied.

He strode toward the confrontation, Seren matching his pace. Behind them, Jorr, Raven, and Aurix followed, forming a united front of Shorling and Dragonkin alike.

"Your Majesty," Pryce called. "Is this how you respond to a Corsair attack? By dividing our forces further?"

"My battlemaster's strategic expertise is needed."

"His 'expertise' guided those Corsair ships to our doorstep," Pryce countered. "We can argue later. Right now, Crystal Shores needs unified defense." He turned to address the gathered defenders directly. "Anyone who cares about this village or Dragonkin honor—to your defense positions! We'll sort loyalties after we survive!"

Perhaps it was the conviction in his voice. Perhaps it was the proximity of the Corsair threat, now visible as black sails on the horizon. Whatever the reason, defenders began moving to their stations, the immediate crisis overriding political division.

Nymeria's expression could have frozen flame. "This isn't over, Harper-Green."

"No," Pryce agreed. "It's just beginning."

As the queen swept away, Thane still in custody but clearly not for long, Pryce turned toward the harbor. The Corsair fleet approached in battle formation, dark ships cutting through Lake Dragontide's morning mist. Signal flags on their masts coordinated their movements—patterns matching exactly what Thane had transmitted from the lighthouse.

"They're following Thane's signal plan precisely," Seren said. "They expect no resistance at the southern breakwater."

Pryce nodded. "Then that's where we'll surprise them. Kai, redirect the Tempest Guardian to the southern approach. Jorr, we need dragons in the air—any who'll follow Seren's command."

"What about Stormwing?" Kai asked.

"Her wing's still healing," Pryce said, though it pained him to admit it. "I won't risk her unless absolutely necessary."

Another projectile whistled overhead, exploding against a warehouse near the docks. Splinters and debris rained down as smoke billowed upward.

They moved toward their positions as the Corsair fleet drew closer. Crystal Shores prepared for battle—a village divided yet united by immediate threat. Dragonkin and Shorling, Royal loyalist and rebel, all faced the same enemy approaching from the west.

The siege of Crystal Shores had begun—and with it, the true test of where loyalties ultimately lay.

CHAPTER 15

Blood-orange light crept across the eastern horizon, illuminating the aftermath of a night without rest. Pryce stood at the harbor's edge, watching Corsair vessels drift just beyond cannon range. After their initial assault, the enemy fleet had withdrawn to a strategic distance.

"They've moved Thane to the Queen's pavilion," Kai reported, appearing at Pryce's side. His face was streaked with soot, his eyes rimmed with exhaustion. "Technically still under guard, but—"

"But we both know how long that will last," Pryce finished.

The division that had begun in the council chamber now infected every aspect of Crystal Shores' defense. Dragonkin loyalists followed Queen Nymeria's orders, establishing separate command structures that often contradicted the village's established protocols. Meanwhile, those who stood with Pryce and Seren—both Shorling and rebel Dragonkin—attempted to maintain a coherent defense with diminishing resources.

"Seren's aerial scouts report unusual activity on the largest Corsair vessel," Kai said. "They're deploying some kind of mechanical harnesses into the water."

"For the seadrakes," Pryce said, recalling the massive creature that had nearly killed them during the first skirmish. "They're preparing their water dragons."

A commotion drew their attention to the village square, where Queen Nymeria had emerged from her pavilion. She moved toward the makeshift prison where Thane was supposedly being held, royal guards clearing her path through gathered villagers.

"The dragon rises as smoke blinds the shepherd." Pipwhistle stood behind them, his cloak of borrowed fabrics fluttering in the morning breeze. Today, the Quibnocket's normally mischievous expression had been replaced by something more urgent.

"Speak plainly for once," Kai said. "We haven't slept in two days."

"The shadow drake breaks free while eyes turn to obvious threats," Pipwhistle clarified, pointing toward a covered wagon near the Queen's pavilion. "The corruption he's cultivated in secret awakens."

"What corruption?" Pryce asked.

Before Pipwhistle could answer, shouts erupted from the direction of Nymeria's pavilion. Guards scattered as something massive burst from beneath the covered wagon—something with scales as black as midnight and eyes that burned with green fire.

"By the depths," Kai whispered. "What is that?"

The creature might once have been a dragon—its basic shape suggested the powerful form of a shadow drake—but corruption had twisted it into something monstrous. Its scales seemed to absorb light rather than reflect it, and where they had been damaged, pulsing veins of toxic green energy were visible beneath. As it spread tattered wings, Pryce could see metal components grafted directly into its flesh, half-mechanical and half-organic.

Atop this abomination sat Thane, free of his restraints, his scales now streaked with the same sickly green that infected his mount.

"He's been keeping it hidden," Pryce said. "All this time."

"Three bloods bound the darkness once," Pipwhistle said, eyes darting to the lake's surface. "Now they seek to unmake what wisdom wove. The ore beneath calls to those who would break The Binding, not knowing what else they might release.

"The corrupted shadow drake launched skyward with unnatural speed, Thane securing himself in a harness that seemed more melded to the creature than strapped upon it. As they climbed, a terrible screeching call echoed across Crystal Shores—a signal that was answered from the water.

The Corsair fleet moved in unison, their formations tightening as dark shapes emerged from the water around them. Seadrakes—at least a dozen—but like Thane's mount, these too had been altered. Metal harnesses encased their heads and spines, with tubes that pulsed with the same toxic green force.

"Binding of Dragon Essence," came Jorr's voice as the young Dragonkin rushed toward them. "It's forbidden magic—extracting a dragon's essence without killing it, leaving the creature enslaved to the wielder's will."

"Can it be stopped?" Pryce asked, watching in horror as the seadrakes began moving in unison—a coordinated attack that no wild creatures could maintain.

"Not easily," Jorr replied. "The binding creates a connection between captor and captured. Breaking one means breaking all—or destroying the source."

Pryce turned toward the stables where Stormwing had been recovering from her injured wing. "We need to evacuate the village. Kai, sound the retreat bells. Everyone to the inland caves as planned."

"And you?" Kai asked.

"Someone needs to buy time. Get them to safety."

"Don't you dare make this some heroic last stand," Kai said. "I've invested too many years in this friendship to have you throw it away on dramatic gestures."

Pryce smiled. "Not planning on dying today. Just need to distract Thane and those seadrakes long enough for the evacuation."

Kai didn't look convinced, but a massive explosion from the harbor demanded his attention. The Corsair fleet had begun its advance, seadrakes clearing a path through Crystal Shores' hastily erected water defenses.

"Go," Pryce said. "Keep my sister safe."

As Kai reluctantly departed, Pryce turned to find Princess Seren landing nearby, her dragon's wings stirring dust as it touched down.

"My mother has ordered all Dragonkin forces to withdraw," she said, dismounting. "She claims Crystal Shores is lost and we must preserve our strength."

"And you're here because . . .?"

"Because some orders deserve to be disobeyed. What's your plan?"

"Get to Stormwing. Take to the air. Distract Thane and his corrupted drake long enough for the village to evacuate."

"That's not a plan," Seren said. "That's a suicide mission."

"Do you have a better idea?"

She didn't. Instead, she gestured to the sky where several dragons circled—those whose riders had chosen to follow her rather than the Queen. "We'll coordinate with you. Four of my best riders can engage the seadrakes while you focus on Thane."

Another explosion rocked the village, closer this time. The Corsair advance was accelerating.

"Be careful," Seren said as Pryce turned to leave. "Thane has embraced magic that corrupts the wielder as much as the victim. He's more dangerous now than ever."

Pryce nodded once before sprinting toward the stables. Around him, Crystal Shores descended into chaos as the evacuation bells began to toll—three short rings, two long, repeated in a pattern that every villager knew meant immediate danger.

He found Stormwing restless, sensing the danger that approached. The storm dragon's injured wing had healed considerably, though Pryce could still see where new scales had formed over damaged tissue.

"Hey, girl," he said softly, approaching with his palm outstretched. "I know you're not fully healed, but we're needed."

Stormwing lowered her massive head, pressing her snout into Pryce's hand. A low rumble vibrated through her chest.

"That's my girl." Pryce stroked her neck. "We've faced worse odds."

As he secured the riding harness, trying to adjust it to avoid putting pressure on her healing wing, a sudden commotion erupted outside. Pryce rushed to the stable entrance to find Dragonkin royal guards surrounding the building.

"By order of Queen Nymeria," their leader announced, "all dragons are to be withdrawn from Crystal Shores immediately."

"Stormwing isn't a Dragonkin mount," Pryce replied. "She's mine."

"All dragons," the guard repeated, his hand moving to his weapon. "The Queen's orders are absolute."

Before Pryce could respond, lightning crackled across the sky—not from Stormwing, but from the approaching battle. The corrupted shadow drake had engaged Seren's loyal riders, green energy clashing with natural dragon fire in spectacular aerial combat.

The distraction was all Pryce needed. He whistled sharply—a signal Stormwing recognized instantly. The storm dragon burst from the stable with explosive force, knocking guards aside as she lowered her shoulder for Pryce to mount. In one fluid motion, he vaulted onto her back, securing himself to the harness as they launched skyward.

The sudden acceleration stole his breath. Despite her injury, Stormwing climbed with power, cutting through ash-laden air as they rose toward the battle above.

The aerial conflict was like nothing Pryce had ever witnessed. Seadrakes twisted through the air, their water-adapted bodies somehow defying gravity as they engaged Seren's dragons. Green energy pulsed along the mechanical harnesses grafted to their bodies, leaving poisonous trails across the sky.

At the center of it all hovered Thane atop his corrupted shadow drake, directing the seadrakes with gestures. The battlemaster had transformed since his escape—his armor now integrated with the same mechanical components that infected his mount, tubes of glowing essence connecting dragon to rider in disturbing symbiosis.

"Pryce!" Seren shouted as her dragon swooped nearby. "The seadrakes are connected to Thane's mount! It's controlling them somehow!"

"Then we take out Thane," Pryce called back, guiding Stormwing into a flanking position.

Seren nodded, banking away to coordinate her remaining riders. Three Dragonkin dragons formed a wedge formation, diving toward the Corsair vessels to disrupt their support fire.

Pryce drew his bow—a weapon he'd rarely used from dragonback—and nocked an arrow. "Get me close, girl. Just one clean shot."

The storm dragon responded, reading his intentions as she always had. They climbed higher, positioning themselves above Thane's corrupted mount, hidden momentarily by a bank of ash clouds.

Then they dove.

Wind screamed past Pryce's ears as Stormwing tucked her wings, plummeting toward their target. The shadow drake sensed their approach too late, beginning to turn as Stormwing extended her wings to stabilize their position.

Pryce drew back his bowstring, sighting along the arrow at Thane's exposed back.

"For Crystal Shores," he whispered, and released.

The arrow flew true—only to disintegrate in midair as it entered the toxic green aura surrounding the shadow drake. Thane turned, his transformed face smiling.

"The dragon-tamer comes to play," he called, his voice distorted by whatever corruption had claimed him. "How fitting that you should witness the fruits of your failure."

Stormwing banked sharply away as the shadow drake lashed out with its tail. Pryce clutched the saddle, adjusting his position to compensate for Stormwing's defensive maneuvers.

"This is what you planned all along," Pryce shouted back. "Using Corsairs as cover for your true purpose—mining the dragon magic ore."

"Not just mining it, boy." Thane guided his mount in a tight circle, keeping pace with

Stormwing's evasive flight. "Activating it. Do you think such power simply waits to be dug from the ground like common metal? No—it requires blood. Dragon blood."

Then Pryce realized what Thane was doing. "The seadrakes. You're draining them to power your machines."

"Efficient, isn't it? The binding technology extracts their essence without killing them—allowing for continuous harvesting." Thane's twisted face showed no remorse. "And soon, we'll have access to the largest dragon magic ore deposit ever discovered—directly beneath your precious village."

Stormwing growled, the sound vibrating through her body and into Pryce's. She sensed his anger and responded with a sudden burst of speed that carried them away from Thane's corrupted drake.

Lightning crackled along Stormwing's scales. As they circled back toward Thane, Pryce felt power building beneath him.

"Now, girl!" he shouted.

Stormwing released a concentrated bolt of electricity that slammed into the shadow drake's side. The creature screeched in pain, its flight pattern faltering momentarily.

But the victory was short-lived. The corruption that had claimed the shadow drake seemed to absorb Stormwing's attack.

"Conventional attacks won't work," Thane called. "This is the future of dragon warfare—bound essence, controlled and amplified."

Below them, the battle for Crystal Shores intensified. Corsair vessels had breached the harbor defenses, their troops swarming onto docks as seadrakes provided aerial support. Seren's loyal riders fought valiantly, but they were outnumbered and outmatched by the coordinated assault.

"Your village falls while you play in the clouds," Thane taunted. "Perhaps I'll build my new command center on the ashes of your family home."

Rage threatened to cloud Pryce's judgment, but he forced it down, analyzing the situation as Stormwing carried him through another evasive pattern. The shadow drake's movements were powerful but predictable—too predictable for a creature known for its agility and cunning.

"The binding is restricting its natural abilities," Pryce realized. "It's stronger but less adaptive."

He leaned forward, stroking Stormwing's neck. "Speed over power. He can't match your natural grace."

Stormwing understood. The storm dragon banked sharply, then executed a complex spiral maneuver that no bound drake could hope to mimic.

As they danced through the air, evading the shadow drake's increasingly frustrated attacks, Pryce spotted a weak point—the connection between Thane's armor and the dragon's harness, where tubes of glowing essence created a bond.

"There," he said, tapping Stormwing's neck to direct her attention. "We need to sever that connection."

They climbed rapidly, putting distance between themselves and their pursuer before looping into position for another diving attack. This time, Pryce didn't reach for his bow. Instead, he drew the hunting knife he kept strapped to his boot—the blade his mother had given him years ago, its edge still sharp enough to slice through scales.

"One pass," he told Stormwing. "Make it count."

The storm dragon tucked her wings again, but this time their dive wasn't directly at Thane. Instead, Stormwing aimed to sweep past the corrupted drake's flank, giving Pryce a chance to strike at the vulnerable tubes as they passed.

They plummeted through ash-laden clouds, emerging directly in the shadow drake's blind spot. The creature sensed them too late, beginning a turn that exposed exactly what Pryce had hoped to reach.

As Stormwing flashed past, her wings extended to stabilize their flight, Pryce leaned out from the saddle—farther than any sane rider would dare—and slashed at the glowing tubes with all his strength.

His blade connected, slicing through one of the connections. Essence sprayed outward, hissing where it touched air. The shadow drake convulsed, its flight pattern disintegrating into chaotic thrashing as the symbiotic link weakened.

Thane howled—not in pain but in rage. "You understand nothing of what you interfere with!" he shouted, fighting to regain control of his mount. "This power will reshape the world!"

"Not my world," Pryce called back, guiding Stormwing into position for another pass.

But before they could attack again, the shadow drake's erratic movements stabilized—not through Thane's control, but through something more sinister. The severed tube had begun to regenerate, knitting it back together.

"You cannot stop what has already begun," Thane said. "The binding grows stronger with each challenge. It adapts. It hungers."

He raised his hands, and the corruption surrounding his mount intensified, spreading outward in tendrils that reached toward the other dragons in the vicinity. Where these tendrils touched, scales darkened, and eyes glazed with momentary confusion.

One of Seren's riders faltered, his mount shuddering as corruption attempted to take hold. The dragon fought against it, screeching in distress as its natural essence battled the magic.

"He's trying to corrupt the other dragons," Pryce realized in horror. "Extend his binding to all of them."

Across the aerial battlefield, Seren had noticed the same phenomenon. She directed her riders to maintain distance from Thane's mount, sacrificing tactical advantage for safety.

"Fall back to secondary positions!" her voice carried across the wind. "Do not engage the shadow drake directly!"

But retreat wasn't an option for Pryce. As long as Thane remained in the air, controlling the seadrakes and spreading corruption, Crystal Shores' evacuation remained in jeopardy.

"One more try," he said to Stormwing. "We need to ground him somehow."

The storm dragon understood, banking into clouds that had darkened. Lightning crackled around them as Stormwing's natural abilities responded to the desperate situation.

As they burst from the cloud cover, electricity arced between Stormwing's wing tips—not a single bolt like before, but a sustained field that surrounded them like a shield.

They dove toward the shadow drake once more, but this time their approach was met with prepared defense. Thane directed his mount to release a stream of corrupted flame—not the natural fire of dragons, but a deadly green inferno that cut through the air between them.

Stormwing barrel-rolled to avoid the worst of it, but part of the flame caught her injured wing. She screeched in pain, her flight pattern faltering as the barely-healed tissue was stressed beyond its limits.

"Steady, girl," Pryce said, shifting his weight to help her compensate. "We can still do this."

For a moment, it seemed they might recover. Stormwing stabilized, her determination outweighing her pain as they prepared for another approach.

Then Thane changed tactics. Instead of pursuing them, the corrupted shadow drake turned its attention toward the village below—particularly the retreating columns of civilians still making their way toward the inland caves.

"No!" Pryce shouted as he realized Thane's intentions.

The shadow drake dove, gathering toxic breath in its mouth as it plummeted toward the helpless evacuees. Thane's laughter carried across the wind—the sound of a man who had embraced madness in his quest for power.

Stormwing responded to Pryce's desperation, tucking her wings to pursue despite her injury. They were fast—faster than the shadow drake's corrupted bulk—but distance and angle worked against them. They wouldn't intercept in time.

"Dive!" came Seren's voice.

Like an avenging spirit, the princess and her dragon flashed past them, placing themselves directly in the shadow drake's path. Her mount released a jet of concentrated flame, forcing Thane to adjust his trajectory.

For a heartbeat, it seemed Seren's intervention had succeeded. The shadow drake swerved, its attack disrupted as it engaged this new threat.

Then everything went wrong.

The corruption surrounding Thane's mount expanded suddenly, enveloping Seren's dragon in lethal energy. The creature faltered, its natural flame choked off as corruption attempted to take hold.

Seren fought to maintain control, her royal training evident in her perfect poise even in crisis. She guided her dragon in a defensive maneuver, breaking away from the corruption's grasp.

But Thane had anticipated this. As Seren's dragon pulled away, the shadow drake lashed out with its tail—not at the dragon, but at Seren herself.

"Seren!" Pryce screamed, urging Stormwing to greater speed.

Time seemed to slow as the corrupted appendage struck the princess. Energy crackled where it connected, spreading through her Dragonkin scales like poison through veins. Seren's back arched in agony, her hands losing their grip on the riding harness as the corruption took hold.

And then she was falling.

Without conscious thought, Pryce directed Stormwing into a desperate dive. The storm dragon responded immediately, ignoring her own pain as she plummeted toward Seren's falling body.

Wind screamed past them as they raced gravity itself. Above, Seren's riderless dragon circled in confusion, unable to help its mistress as corruption continued to spread across its scales.

"Faster," Pryce urged, though Stormwing was already giving everything she had.

They reached Seren mere seconds before she would have struck the ground. Stormwing extended her talons with surgical precision, catching the princess's armor without puncturing flesh beneath. The sudden deceleration nearly tore Pryce from the saddle, but he clung to the harness.

With Seren secured in her grasp, Stormwing pulled out of the dive, wings straining against the combined weight. For a terrifying moment, Pryce thought they might crash regardless—but the storm dragon's determination matched his own. They leveled out just above the treetops, Stormwing's wing beats slow and labored as she carried them toward the village center.

Thane's mocking laughter followed them, but the battlemaster did not pursue. He had accomplished enough—demonstrating his power, spreading fear, and striking a critical blow against their leadership.

As they landed in the village square, Pryce saw the corruption spreading across Seren's body. Elemental power pulsed beneath her scales, following the natural patterns but twisting them into something wrong. Her breathing came in shallow gasps.

"Help!" Pryce shouted as he gathered the princess in his arms. "I need healers!"

Kai appeared from the chaos, taking in Seren's condition. "What happened?"

"Thane's corruption," Pryce explained, laying Seren carefully on a makeshift pallet that someone had hurriedly provided. "It's spreading through her scales."

The corrupted energy had reached Seren's neck, crawling upward toward her face. Where it passed, her natural scale patterns darkened.

"We need both traditions," Jorr said, appearing beside them. "Shorling medicine for the physical trauma, Dragonkin healing for the corruption."

Dr. Bennett pushed through the crowd, his medical bag clutched tightly in his hands. Behind him came a Dragonkin healer—one of Seren's loyal followers who had defied the Queen's withdrawal order.

"Clear space," the doctor commanded. "And someone bring clean water—boiled, mind you!"

The Dragonkin healer knelt beside Seren, her scaled hands hovering over the spreading corruption. "This is ancient magic. Binding magic turned inward. It seeks to enslave her essence as it does the dragons."

"Can you stop it?" Pryce asked.

The healer's expression was grim. "I can try to slow it, but this corruption comes from forbidden knowledge. It may be beyond my skills alone."

As they worked to stabilize Seren, Kai pulled Pryce aside. "The evacuation is almost complete, but the Corsairs have taken the harbor. Thane's corruption is spreading to more dragons—even some of ours are showing signs of infection."

Another explosion rocked the village. The ground beneath their feet trembled, but not from the impact.

"Something's happening," Kai said, glancing down. "The ground's been shaking like this for the past hour, getting stronger each time."

"The ore," Pryce realized. "Thane said it needed to be activated by dragon blood. The corruption he's spreading—it's affecting the deposits beneath us."

A crack appeared in the square's paving stones, widening as they watched.

"We need to get her out of here," Pryce said, turning back to where the healers worked frantically. "The whole village could be unstable if the ore deposits are being activated."

"There's more," Kai said. "Faye sent a message from the caves. The lake water near the shore has started to glow with the same light. Whatever's happening, it's affecting the whole region."

Pryce looked to the sky where Thane's corrupted shadow drake still circled, noxious energy trailing from its form like a banner of conquest. Other dragons fought in the distance— Seren's loyal riders against seadrakes and newly corrupted mounts.

"This is just the beginning," Pryce said. "Thane's using the corruption to break the ancient Binding that sealed the ore deposits."

"And if he succeeds?"

Before Pryce could answer, Seren gasped, as a fresh wave of corruption pulsed through her body. The healer murmured incantations while Dr. Bennett administered some herbal concoction, but the corruption continued its relentless advance.

"We're losing her," the doctor said.

Pryce knelt beside Seren, taking her hand despite the corruption that threatened to spread to him. "Hold on. We'll find a way to stop this."

Her eyes opened, finding his with effort. "The Binding," she whispered, her voice barely audible. "It's the key to everything. My mother . . . she wants to break it completely."

"Save your strength," Pryce told her.

"No." Seren's grip tightened on his hand. "Listen. The ore can't be fully extracted while the Binding holds. Three bloodlines . . . three keys . . . your family is one of them."

Another tremor shook the ground, stronger than before. Cracks spread across the village square.

"Find the ancient guardians," Seren whispered, her consciousness fading as corruption reached her jawline. "Before it's too late."

Her hand went limp in his. Not dead—her chest still rose and fell with shallow breaths—but lost to unconsciousness as the corruption continued its spread.

Pryce rose and looked to the sky, where Thane still commanded his corrupted forces. The battle for Crystal Shores had transformed into something far more dangerous—a fight not just for a village, but for ancient powers that should never have been disturbed.

CHAPTER 16

Pryce knelt beside Seren, the princess's skin growing paler as corruption spread through her scales. The green tendrils pulsed beneath her skin, creeping toward her face. Around them, Crystal Shores crumbled—buildings aflame, the harbor occupied by Corsair forces, and above it all, Thane's corrupted shadow drake circling like a harbinger of doom.

"We need to move her," Dr. Bennett said, pressing a poultice against the worst of her wounds. "The ground beneath us isn't stable."

As if to emphasize his point, another tremor shook the village square, cracks spider-webbing through the stones. Behind them, the Dragonkin healer said incantations that seemed to slow but not stop the corruption's advance.

Pryce took Seren's limp hand. He thought of her final words before losing consciousness: *Three bloodlines . . . three keys . . . your family is one of them.*

"What does it mean?" he whispered.

A sudden warmth against his thigh startled him. He reached into his pocket and found the source—the wooden token Pipwhistle had given him days ago, now almost as hot as coal fresh from the fire. As he drew it out, the wood's surface began to change before his eyes, the outer bark-like layer cracking and peeling away to reveal metal beneath. The newly exposed surface gleamed with an inner light that hadn't been there before, ancient runes appearing along its edge, shimmering blue against the bronze core.

"The Watcher's Mark awakens." Pipwhistle stood beside him, his patchwork cloak unusually still in the chaos around them. The Quibnocket's eyes fixed on the glowing coin.

"What is this?" Pryce asked.

"A key forgotten by most, remembered by few." Pipwhistle pointed at the emerging runes. "Your bloodline guarded this for generations. The Harper-Greens were chosen as Shorling representatives at The Binding."

Another tremor, stronger than before. In the harbor, a Corsair vessel unleashed a barrage against the remaining defenders.

"The Binding," Pryce repeated, his mind racing back to Old Finnegan's explanation. "The magical treaty that sealed the ore deposits."

"Not just a treaty," Pipwhistle said. "A protection against the very corruption you now witness." He gestured to Seren's spreading

234

affliction, then to the sky where corrupted dragons wheeled. "What was bound together cannot be broken without consequence."

The coin pulsed in Pryce's palm, growing warmer when he turned it toward the center of the village square. "It's responding. Like it wants to go somewhere."

"The key seeks its lock," Pipwhistle said. "Three bloodlines, three keys. When darkness rises, the three must join again."

Understanding dawned. "It can lead us to the original Binding site."

Kai appeared through the smoke, his face streaked with soot and blood. "Pryce, we can't hold the western approach much longer. Thane's corruption is spreading to more dragons."

"Help me with Seren," Pryce said. "This coin—it's one of the keys to The Binding. It might be our only chance to stop Thane."

Skepticism flashed across Kai's face.

"Are you mad?" Dr. Bennett protested, stepping between them and Seren. "She needs medical attention, not to be dragged across a battlefield on some token-chasing adventure!"

The Dragonkin healer looked up from her incantations. "The princess's condition is critical. Moving her could accelerate the corruption's spread."

"And staying here will kill her for certain," Pryce countered, showing them the glowing token.

"This is connected to The Binding—the ancient magic created to counter corruption. It might be her only chance."

Another violent tremor shook the ground beneath them, widening the cracks in the village square. Nearby, a building collapsed in a shower of sparks and debris.

"We don't have time to debate," Pryce said. "The corruption is spreading, the ground is becoming unstable, and Corsairs are advancing. This token is responding to something—something that might save not just Seren but all of us."

Dr. Bennett exchanged glances with the Dragonkin healer, both recognizing the desperate situation.

"Fine," the doctor relented. "But I'm coming with you. And you," he pointed to the Dragonkin healer, "bring your herbs and whatever else you need."

Kai looked at the flimsy makeshift pallet Seren was lying on. "This won't survive the journey," he said, quickly scanning their surroundings. He spotted a sturdy wooden door that had been blown from its hinges in a nearby explosion. "That will work better."

He dragged the door over, positioning it alongside Seren's pallet. Together with a young Shorling volunteer who'd been assisting Dr. Bennett, they carefully transferred the unconscious princess onto the more substantial makeshift stretcher.

"Lead the way," Kai said to Pryce, taking the front end of the door while the volunteer grabbed the back. "But make it quick—doors weren't designed for transport?"

"Which way?" asked the young volunteer.

Pryce extended his hand, watching as the coin's glow intensified when pointed toward the oldest building in the village—the stone meeting hall that predated Crystal Shores itself.

"There."

***

The ancient meeting hall stood remarkably untouched amidst the battle, as if protected by forces beyond the visible. Inside, Pryce followed the coin's guidance, its warmth increasing as they approached the central hearth containing a massive stone circle.

"The original village was built around this hearth," Pryce said, remembering Finnegan's tales. "Before Crystal Shores even had a name."

The coin burned almost too hot to hold now. Pryce knelt beside the cold hearth, searching for . . . something. Anything.

"There's nothing here," Kai said as he and the volunteer carefully set down the stretcher bearing Seren. "Just old stones."

But Pryce felt it—a pull, a certainty. He pressed the coin against the central stone, and the effect was immediate. Blue light blazed from the token, spreading between the hearth stones like liquid fire, illuminating ancient carving previously invisible.

The entire hearth circle began to shift, stones grinding against one another as they rotated and reconfigured. Then, with a final groan of ancient mechanisms, the center opened, revealing stone steps descending into darkness.

"By the lake's depths," Kai said, eyes wide.

Pipwhistle appeared on the staircase, holding a torch that cast eerie shadows. "The way opens for blood of the binding. What slumbered now awakens."

They maneuvered the stretcher down the narrow stairs with difficulty, Kai taking most of the weight while the volunteer guided the rear. Entering a circular chamber beneath the village. Ancient torches sprung to life as they entered, revealing walls covered in elaborate murals depicting three races: Shorlings, dragons, and figures with scales who could only be early Dragonkin.

At the chamber's center stood a triangular altar, each corner marked with a distinct symbol: a stylized wave for Shorlings, a flame for dragons, and a scaled hand for Dragonkin.

"The binding chamber," Pipwhistle said. "Where three became one to protect what lies beneath."

Pryce approached the altar, the coin pulling toward the Shorling corner as if drawn by a magnet. A small depression in the stone matched the coin's dimensions perfectly.

"The first key," he said, placing the token in position.

It sank into the stone with a soft click, blue light spreading through channels carved into the altar. But the light only filled one-third of the triangle, stopping abruptly.

"Three keys," Kai said. "We only have one."

Pryce looked at Seren, corruption now reaching her temples. "Seren said my family was one of the three bloodlines. The Harper-Greens represent the Shorlings. That leaves Dragonkin and dragons."

"And how exactly do we get keys from them?" Kai asked. "The one Dragonkin who might help us is dying, and I don't think dragons carry spare keys around their necks."

A low rumble shook the chamber—not from the unstable ground above, but from the staircase entrance. Stormwing's massive head appeared, the storm dragon somehow managing to squeeze her bulk into the passage.

"Stormwing," Pryce said, relief flooding through him. "How did you—"

The dragon's eyes fixed on the altar, recognizing something beyond Shorling understanding. She extended her neck, touching her snout to the corner marked with the dragon symbol.

Blue lightning crackled between her scales, flowing into the altar. The second section of the triangle illuminated.

"She is the key," Pryce realized. "Not a physical token—her essence, her blood. The dragon bloodline itself."

The altar hummed with energy, two-thirds now alight. But the final corner—the Dragonkin section—remained dark.

"Seren," Pryce said, turning to the princess. "She needs to connect with the third position."

"She's unconscious," Kai pointed out. "And corrupted. How can she—"

"The Binding was created to counter corruption," Pryce said, remembering Finnegan's words. "If we can complete the circuit, maybe it will purify her as well."

With Kai's help, Pryce carried Seren to the altar, positioning her hand over the Dragonkin corner. Nothing happened.

"It's not working," Kai said. Above them, sounds of battle grew louder.

Pryce looked at his own hand, at the faint scales. "I have both bloodlines in me. Shorling from birth, Dragonkin from transformation."

"You can't risk touching that corruption," Kai protested. "It'll spread to you."

"If I don't, we all die anyway." Pryce took a deep breath. "Three bloodlines must join. I'll be the bridge."

Before Kai could stop him, Pryce placed his hand over Seren's, pressing both their palms against the final corner.

Pain exploded through his arm as corruption leapt eagerly from Seren's scales to his. Green tendrils shot up his wrist, racing toward his heart. But alongside it came something else—brilliant blue energy from the activated portions of the altar, flowing to Pryce.

Two forces warred within him, one destroying, one healing. Pryce gritted his teeth, focusing on the connection, on completing the circuit.

"Hold on, don't let go," Kai said. "I think it's working!"

With a final surge of will, Pryce pushed through the pain, focusing on his hand against Seren's on the altar, on The Binding it represented. *Protection, not destruction. Unity, not division.*

The third corner blazed to life. The triangle completed, power surging through the entire altar. A column of purifying blue light erupted upward, piercing through the chamber ceiling, through the meeting hall floor, shooting skyward like a beacon.

The corruption in Pryce's arm receded, driven back by cleansing energy. He watched in amazement as the same happened to Seren—toxic energy expelled from her body in wisps of dissipating smoke, her natural scale patterns restoring to their original luster.

"It worked," Kai said.

The chamber trembled, not with destructive force but with awakening power. The murals on the wall began to glow, depicting the original Binding ceremony—representatives of three races standing as they were now, channeling protective magic into the depths of the lake.

"The Binding strengthens," Pipwhistle said. "What was weakened now fortifies."

Above them, through the shaft of light, they could hear screams—not of pain but of liberation. The corrupted dragons were being cleansed, Thane's control broken by the surging power of the original Binding.

Seren's eyes snapped open. She looked at Pryce, at their joined hands, understanding dawning.

"You found it," she whispered. "The original Binding site."

"Your words led us here," Pryce said. "Three bloodlines, three keys."

The princess struggled to sit up, her strength returning as corruption fled her body. "The light . . . they'll see it throughout the village. Above the village."

"Good," Pryce said. "Let them see what true power looks like."

***

They emerged from the chamber into chaos transformed. The column of blue light pierced the clouds, visible for miles across Lake Dragontide. Rain had begun to fall—not the toxic ash that had filled the air before, but clean, purifying water that hissed where it touched corrupted scales and machinery.

Warriors on both sides had paused, transfixed by the supernatural display. On the battlements, Dragonkin who had fought for Nymeria now lowered their weapons in confusion and awe. Among the Corsair ships, seadrakes thrashed as control mechanisms failed, many breaking free entirely to plunge back into the lake's depths.

Thane's shadow drake circled the light column, screeching as its corruption destabilized. The battlemaster could be seen fighting to maintain control, the mechanical components fused to his armor shorting out in the cleansing rain.

"The tide turns," Seren said, standing on her own power now. "My mother will not expect this."

Queen Nymeria appeared at the head of her royal guard, walking through the battlefield toward the meeting hall. Her face twisted with fury when she saw Seren standing with Pryce and Kai.

"What have you done?" she demanded, looking at the column of light.

"Restored what you sought to break. The Binding protects us all, mother—even from ourselves."

"Foolish child. That power belongs to the Dragonkin alone. These Shorlings are unworthy to—"

"The Binding was created by all three races," Pryce interrupted. "It belongs to none alone and all together."

Nymeria's gaze shifted to him, hatred cold in her eyes. "The half-blood speaks of matters beyond his understanding. The ore beneath this village is Dragonkin birthright."

"Your Majesty," one of her guards called, pointing skyward. "The shadow drake—it fails!"

Above them, Thane's mount shuddered mid-air, corruption visibly burning away. The battlemaster fought to maintain altitude.

Nymeria watched the situation. Her forces divided, her plan unraveling, the tide of battle visibly turning against her.

"This is not over," she said, backing toward her remaining loyal guards. "Crystal Shores sits upon power you cannot comprehend. We will return."

"You'll find us waiting," Pryce said. "With The Binding restored and strengthened."

A shout from the harbor drew their attention. The Corsair flagship had begun to pull away, other vessels following its retreat. On its deck stood a figure Pryce hadn't seen before—a captain with a crimson-edged cutlass raised in defiance.

"Captain Redblade," Seren identified him. "The Corsair commander."

"And Thane's cousin," added Pipwhistle, appearing suddenly beside them. "Blood bound to blood in treachery's embrace."

This revelation sent whispers rippling through nearby Dragonkin warriors. Family ties explained the coordination between forces that should have been enemies.

Thane's shadow drake plummeted toward the Corsair flagship, no longer capable of sustained flight. The battlemaster leapt from his failing mount to the ship's deck, corruption still clinging to his armor in patches. He exchanged brief words with Redblade before both disappeared below deck.

"They're retreating," Kai said, watching the Corsair fleet turning westward.

Nymeria backed further away, her loyal guards forming a protective circle. "Remember this moment, daughter," she called to Seren. "When you chose Shorlings over your own blood."

"I chose honor over ambition, mother," Seren replied. "As a true Dragonkin should."

With a final furious glare, Nymeria retreated with her remaining forces toward the royal ships docked on the eastern harbor. Those Dragonkin who remained—those who had witnessed The Binding's restoration—looked to Seren with newfound respect, many dropping to one knee in the ancient gesture of Dragonkin fealty.

The column of light began to fade, its purpose fulfilled. As it receded, Pryce felt a warmth against his chest. Reaching into his shirt, he found the wooden-turned-metal token had somehow returned to him, traveling from the chamber below through the column of light. When he examined it, he saw it had changed—now marked permanently with all three symbols of The Binding interlocked: wave, flame, and scaled hand.

Across Crystal Shores, corruption continued to dissipate under the cleansing rain. Dragons freed from Thane's control landed among the defenders, disoriented but no longer hostile. The seadrakes had vanished back into Lake Dragontide's depths.

"It's over," Kai said, dropping to sit on the meeting hall steps, exhaustion finally claiming him.

"This battle," Pryce corrected, pocketing the transformed coin. "Not the war."

Seren addressed the gathered Dragonkin warriors. "Those who recognize the truth of The Binding and wish to honor our ancestors' wisdom, stand with me now. Those who cannot, join my mother—but know this: today we witnessed why The Binding was created. Not to constrain our power, but to protect us from its corruption."

Nearly two-thirds of the remaining Dragonkin moved to her side, including Raven,

Aurix, and Jorr. They formed a line facing Crystal Shores' defenders—not in opposition but in alliance.

Pryce extended his hand to Seren. The princess took it without hesitation, their joined hands raised for all to see.

"Crystal Shores stands," Pryce called out to Shorlings and Dragonkin alike. "Not through conquest or control, but through the wisdom of our ancestors who knew that separate, we fall prey to corruption; together, we stand against all threats."

The cheers began slowly, exhausted voices finding strength in victory. Shorlings and Dragonkin raised weapons together, united by shared battle and the mysterious power they had witnessed.

As the rain continued to fall, washing away blood and corruption, Stormwing bumped her massive head against Pryce's shoulder, a gesture of affection.

"We did it, girl," Pryce said softly, running his hand along her rain-slicked scales. The storm had broken. The tide had turned. And though enemies retreated rather than surrendered, future battles surely awaited.

Pryce looked toward the western horizon where Corsair ships shrank to distant specks. Somewhere out there, Thane and Redblade nursed their wounds and plotted revenge. Queen Nymeria's royal vessels vanished around the eastern headland, her ambitions temporarily thwarted.

"What happens now?" Kai asked.

"Now, we build something new from something very old."

The sun broke through rain clouds, casting golden light across the battered village. And for the first time in days, it felt like a beginning rather than an end.

CHAPTER 17

Seven days had passed since the battle, since The Binding had been restored. The village showed signs of both destruction and remarkable renewal.

Pryce walked along the shoreline, cataloging the changes with each step. Buildings still stood blackened and broken in some areas, yet around them, plant life flourished with vigor—wildflowers pushing through cracks in the stone, vines reclaiming damaged walls. The lake water itself seemed different, clearer somehow, with a subtle luminescence where it lapped against the shore.

"The Binding's influence," Old Man Finnegan had explained when Pryce first noticed the phenomenon. "Balance returning to what was unbalanced."

As he approached the village center, Pryce heard the now-familiar sound of friendly bickering coming from the infirmary—a building that had survived the battle relatively intact. Inside, Dr.

Bennett and the Dragonkin healer Iradis stood on opposite sides of Seren's bed.

"Cold compresses for scale inflammation," Iradis insisted "This is basic healing practice among Dragonkin."

"Warmth improves circulation and speeds healing," Dr. Bennett countered, holding up a heated stone wrap. "Principles of medicine don't change just because your patient has scales."

"Perhaps," Seren suggested from her bed, looking more amused than pained, "if you two stopped trying to out-heal each other, you might notice your patient is already recovered enough to be thoroughly annoyed by both of you."

Both healers turned to her in surprise. Seren sat upright.

"The princess makes a valid observation," Iradis admitted.

"Indeed," Dr. Bennett agreed, then paused. "Though perhaps a combination approach . . ." He offered the heated stones to Iradis, who placed them strategically before applying her cooling salve around them.

Seren caught Pryce's eye and gave a slight eye-roll. "Seven days of this," she said. "If the corruption didn't kill me, their combined fussing might."

"You look stronger today," Pryce said, moving to stand beside her bed.

"Strong enough to join the council proceedings rather than having them parade through my sickroom," she said. "Any news?"

"Reconstruction continues. The Dragonkin engineers you sent for arrived yesterday—they're already helping reinforce the harbor."

"And my mother?"

Pryce hesitated. "A messenger arrived this morning. Formal acknowledgment of temporary withdrawal, but reaffirming Dragonkin claims to what lies beneath Crystal Shores."

"Of course she did. This isn't over, Pryce. She's simply regrouping."

"I know." He touched the metal token that now hung on a leather cord around his neck.

A commotion outside interrupted them— shouts from the harbor, not of alarm but excitement. Pryce made his way to the window. In the distance, a ship approached, flying both Oceanrider and Shorling banners.

"My parents," Pryce said, recognizing the vessel. "They're back."

***

The reunions at the harbor overflowed with emotions—joy, relief, confusion. The Oceanrider reinforcements that Tyler and Ellie had secured from Port Ravenspur arrived to find a battle already won, a village damaged but standing, and most

251

shocking of all, Dragonkin and Shorlings working side by side in recovery efforts.

"I leave for a while," Tyler said, embracing Pryce firmly, "and you rewrite centuries of history."

Ellie hugged him next, tears glistening in her eyes. "When we heard about the Corsair fleet, we were terrified we wouldn't make it back in time."

"It was . . . complicated," Pryce said, the understatement pulling a laugh from Kai, who stood nearby with his arm in a sling—a souvenir from the battle.

As preparations began for a formal council meeting to bring the newcomers up to speed, Pryce found himself pulled aside by his father. Tyler guided him toward a quiet section of the dock, away from the bustle of unloading supplies.

"So," Tyler began, a curious expression on his face, "I'm hearing some interesting stories about recent events."

"I'm sure you are."

"Stories about some kind of, ah, altercation at the Rusty Anchor." Tyler crossed his arms, attempting a serious expression. "You wouldn't happen to know anything about that, would you?"

Pryce shifted uncomfortably. "It was a minor incident."

"Minor?" Tyler raised an eyebrow. "From what I hear, half the tavern's furniture ended up in splinters."

"That's an exaggeration."

"I'm told you were involved in a . . . how did they put it? A 'diplomatic incident of unprecedented proportions.'"

Pryce sighed. "It wasn't like that."

"Then what was it like?"

After a moment's hesitation, Pryce explained about Drakonir's insults, the rising tension, and the final slur against Stormwing that had pushed him past endurance.

Tyler listened intently, his expression shifting from stern to puzzled to something Pryce couldn't quite read. When the story concluded, he was quiet for a long moment.

"So you're telling me," Tyler finally said, "that you risked a diplomatic incident, endangered an alliance, and started a brawl that nearly destroyed the tavern . . . all because someone insulted your dragon?"

Pryce braced himself for disappointment. "A Shorling's first and final duty is to their dragon."

A pause stretched between them. Then Tyler's serious expression cracked. "Good for you, son."

"What?"

"Some things are worth fighting for. Honor, principles . . . and those we care about, scales and all."

"You're not angry?"

"How could I be?" Tyler laughed. "You're your mother's son. You should have seen her the time someone insulted our first fishing boat. I thought we'd need to rebuild the entire harbor tavern." His expression grew more serious. "Leading isn't just about making perfect decisions, Pryce. It's about standing for what matters, even when it's difficult. Especially then."

As they walked back toward the village center, Pryce felt something shift between them. He was no longer simply Tyler's son, but a leader in his own right, with his own path to forge.

***

The Great Hall hummed with conversation, its roof newly repaired and its walls bearing fresh marks from the battle. Representatives from Crystal Shores, the Oceanrider fleet, and the Dragonkin delegation filled the space.

Mayor Wright stood at the head of the newly crafted triangular table, specifically designed to have no head position. Shorlings occupied one side, Dragonkin another, and the third remained open for those who represented both, or neither.

"The Binding Council," the mayor announced, gesturing to the three carved chairs set at each point of the triangle. "Three representatives with equal authority, as it was in ancient times. The Shorling voice, the Dragonkin voice, and the Dragon-keeper's voice."

Later, after detailed accounts of the battle had been shared and preliminary reconstruction plans approved, Pryce glanced at his father seated among the council members, catching Tyler's eye.

Tyler studied him for a moment, then gave an almost imperceptible nod—not permission, but recognition.

Pryce rose, the wooden floor creaking beneath his boots as the assembly quieted.

"The Binding has been restored," he said. "But our work is just beginning. The corruption we faced revealed weaknesses in our separation—ancient knowledge forgotten, skills divided rather than shared."

He took a deep breath. "I propose we formalize Island of Emberfall as a permanent sanctuary where dragons, Dragonkin, and Shorlings can learn from each other. With proper support, it could become a center for healing, for training, for rebuilding what was lost."

To his surprise, it was Seren who spoke next, rising despite her still-healing injuries. "As representative of the remaining Dragonkin force, I support this proposal." Whispers rippled through her delegation—many had expected her to return to Dragonkin territories. "Furthermore, I offer my services as co-developer of this sanctuary."

The debate that followed was spirited. Questions of resources, governance, and access were raised and addressed.

As the assembly began to disperse following Pryce's proposal, Seren approached him. "Your idea to formalize the santuary was unexpected. Like many things that have happened between our peoples."

Pryce nodded, aware of curious glances from those nearby. "Speaking of unexpected, what of our betrothal? It was arranged to seal an alliance that no longer exists—at least not in the way Queen Nymeria intended."

Seren smiled. "I believe the terms were 'sealed in the traditional manner through marriage.' But nothing specified when such a marriage must take place. "Perhaps . . . perhaps the betrothal could remain, but on our terms. Not as a political arrangement, but as a possibility to be explored when we're ready—if we're ever ready."

Pryce felt an unexpected lightness in his chest. "So we remain formally betrothed, but with the understanding that we decide our own timing?"

"And our own hearts. My mother will be furious, of course. But she can hardly object to us adhering to the exact letter of the agreement."

"I can think of worse fates than remaining betrothed to you."

"As can I," she replied. "Though I expect we'll have our hands quite full with this sanctuary of yours."

"Ours," Pryce corrected. "If you're staying."

"I am. Some paths, once chosen, cannot be abandoned—even when they lead somewhere unexpected."

"So," Kai said, approaching them. "Emberfall Sanctuary becomes official. From half-finished project to diplomatic centerpiece. Not bad for a pile of rocks in the middle of the lake."

"Speaking of projects," Pryce said, "I hear you've been busy at the forge."

Kai shrugged, then winced as the movement jostled his injured arm. "Just some experiments. The traditional dragon harnesses chafe their scales raw over time. I figured there might be a better way."

"Your father must be pleased to have you back at the smithy."

"He's pretending to be annoyed, but I caught him showing my designs to Jorr yesterday." Kai grinned. "Turns out blacksmithing for dragons requires some adjustments. The first saddle fitting nearly set his beard on fire when Emberstriker got excited."

Outside the Great Hall, the afternoon sun illuminated an unusual scene. A group of Dragonkin warriors stood at the harbor's edge, awkwardly attempting to cast fishing nets under the instruction of elderly Shorling fishermen. Nearby, several village elders struggled through a Dragonkin scale-care demonstration, their tongues tripping over unfamiliar terms.

"You're saying it wrong," a young Dragonkin corrected. "It's 'Kresshar'vek'—the joint where the wing connects to the shoulder."

"Kresh-ver-kek," the Shorling elder attempted, resulting in a burst of laughter from the Dragonkin.

"You just said 'pickled toe fungus,'" the young Dragonkin explained, wiping tears from his eyes.

"Well, how was I supposed to know? Your language sounds like someone choking on a fishbone."

"And yours sounds like water bubbling through mud. Let's try again."

Pryce watched the exchange with quiet satisfaction. Not perfect understanding, perhaps, but something more valuable—the willingness to try, to laugh at mistakes rather than take offense, to begin the long process of learning each other's ways.

***

Two weeks after the battle, Emberfall bustled with activity. The rocky outcropping that had once housed a neglected outpost now sprouted fresh construction—expanded paddocks for recovering dragons, a proper infirmary combining Shorling and Dragonkin healing techniques, and training areas where riders from both traditions could learn from each other.

Pryce stood on the highest point of the island, Stormwing lounging beside him in the warm sunlight. The dragon had fully recovered, her injured wing now stronger than before. From this vantage point, Pryce could see the entire sanctuary taking shape below.

"It's coming along faster than I expected," Seren said, joining him at the overlook. She moved with increasing ease, though a faint silver line along her jawline remained as a permanent reminder of the corruption she had survived.

"People are eager to build something new," Pryce said.

"Or rebuild something very old." She gestured to the triangular building being constructed at the island's center—a small replica of ancient Binding chambers like the one beneath Crystal Shores.

They stood in comfortable silence, watching the activity below. Workers moved between projects—Shorling carpenters alongside Dragonkin stonemasons, dragon handlers consulting on paddock designs, healers comparing notes on treatment methods.

"My mother will return," Seren said after a while, eyes fixed on the distant horizon. "Not today, perhaps not this season, but eventually. The ore is too valuable to abandon."

"And when she does?"

"We'll be ready." Seren touched her own scaled cheek. "What happened here, what we discovered together—it matters, Pryce. The Binding isn't just some ancient treaty. It's protection against our worst instincts. Against corruption that lives in all of us."

Their conversation was interrupted by the distinctive sound of hammer on metal. In a clearing below, Kai had established a temporary forge. The one-armed blacksmith worked alongside his father and Jorr, shaping what appeared to be metal components for dragon harnesses. As they watched, Kai held up a curved piece for inspection, its design clearly intended to work with a dragon's natural contours.

"He has a gift," Seren observed. "Traditional Dragonkin metalwork is beautiful but often impractical. His designs actually consider the dragon's comfort."

"Kai has always been good at seeing practical solutions," Pryce said. "Just don't tell him I said that, his ego is big enough already."

A fluttering of wings announced a messenger—not one of Faye's gulls, but a small jewel-toned bird Pryce didn't recognize. It landed on Seren's outstretched finger, delivering a tiny scroll case.

"From the eastern ranges," she said after reading the message. "The first of the dragons born after The Binding's restoration are showing . . . unusual characteristics."

"What kind of characteristics?"

"Crystal-like patterns in their scales. Enhanced sensing abilities. The hatchlings appear drawn to water in ways uncommon for mountain-dwelling dragons." Seren rolled the message thoughtfully between her fingers. "Changes are coming."

Before they could discuss it further, a voice interrupted from behind. "When old magic wakes, the world reshapes itself to match."

Pryce turned to find Pipwhistle perched improbably on Stormwing's tail. The Quibnocket's patchwork cloak seemed to contain even more scraps of fabric than before, and his wiry hair stood out in all directions like a thistle bloom.

"Pipwhistle," Pryce said, surprised. "I thought you'd disappeared after the battle."

"Quibnockets never disappear," the small figure corrected. "We merely step sideways until needed again."

"And you're needed now?" Seren asked, studying the strange being with curiosity.

"Perhaps. Perhaps not." Pipwhistle hopped down, producing a small leather cylinder from within his cloak. "But this certainly is."

He handed the cylinder to Pryce, who opened it to reveal an ancient scroll, its edges worn but the text still legible—written in a script that combined Shorling letters with Dragonkin runes.

"From before the division," Pipwhistle explained. "When knowledge flowed freely between peoples. Wisdom about dragons, about The Binding, about what sleeps beneath the lake."

The Quibnocket's expression grew solemn. "The Binding was created to protect more than ore deposits, young Harper-Green. Ancient guardians lie in the deepest waters—neither fully awake nor truly sleeping. The Binding keeps them . . . content."

"Nightfathom," Pryce whispered, remembering Finnegan's tales. "The legendary dragon said to slumber beneath Lake Dragontide's depths."

"And others like him. Primordial forces from the world's beginning. The recent disturbances have . . . stirred them."

"Is that a warning?" Seren asked.

"A truth. Neither more nor less. But that's a concern for another time!" Pipwhistle turned to Pryce. "Your mother sent me, you know."

"My mother?"

"Well, not directly. Old connections from her adventures recognized your need. The Harper women have a knack for finding trouble worth getting into." Pipwhistle grinned. "You have her eyes. Her spirit too."

With that statement, the Quibnocket backed toward the cliff edge.

"Will we see you again?" Pryce asked.

"When next the three worlds tremble." Pipwhistle teetered on the brink. "Watch the water for shadows, young Binding-keeper. Not all that wakes wishes well." And with that, he tipped backward off the cliff.

Pryce rushed to the edge, but there was no sign of Pipwhistle, only the gently lapping waves below.

"Well," Seren said after a moment, "that was . . ."

"Typical," Pryce finished with a wry smile. "According to my mother, at least."

***

On the evening marking three weeks since the battle, a small ceremony gathered at Crystal Shores' harbor. The Swiftwind, once abandoned and half-sunk, now floated proudly at dock, its hull repaired and reinforced. Only one element remained to complete the restoration.

"Ready?" Kai called from the dock, where he stood beside a covered shape.

Pryce nodded from the ship's bow, securing the mounting bracket. Together with Tyler and two Dragonkin helpers, they carefully raised the newly carved figurehead into position. As the covering fell away, gasps and appreciative cheers rose from the gathered crowd.

The wooden storm dragon figurehead that Pryce had begun carving weeks ago now bore little resemblance to his original design. The wooden core remained—graceful neck extended and wings swept back—but now metal elements enhanced the carving. Silver-white metal outlined each scale, bronze traced the wing membranes, and steel reinforced the claws. Where wood and metal joined, the lines flowed seamlessly, one medium enhancing rather than dominating the other.

Most striking of all, at the dragon's chest, three symbols had been inlaid in contrasting materials—the wave, flame, and scaled hand of The Binding, interlocking in perfect balance.

"It's beautiful," Ellie said, standing at Pryce's side as the final bolts were secured. "Your carving and Kai's metalwork—neither would be as striking alone."

"That's rather the point," Pryce said, running his hand along the smooth surface where wood and metal merged.

As the evening deepened, lanterns were lit along the harbor, illuminating the mixed fleet that now protected Crystal Shores—Shorling fishing vessels retrofitted with defensive capabilities, the repaired Oceanrider ship Tempest Guardian, and two sleek Dragonkin patrol boats. Above, dragons circled on evening patrol—Stormwing's distinctive silhouette leading three others in formation.

Pryce made his way to the shoreline, away from the celebration. The metal token hung against his chest. He gazed out across Lake Dragontide's dark waters, wondering what truly lay in its deepest trenches. Were Nightfathom and other ancient guardians truly stirring? What would it mean if they woke completely?

He felt rather than heard Seren approach, her presence now familiar enough that it no longer startled him.

"Contemplating our next crisis?" she asked, following his gaze to the horizon where stars met water.

"Is it strange that part of me misses it? Not the danger, but the clarity of purpose."

Seren smiled. "Not strange at all. Battle makes choices simple—survive, protect, prevail. Peace is more complex."

"Speaking of complexity," Pryce said, producing a sealed message tube from his pocket. "Our scouts report increased Corsair activity near the Stormshroud Isles. And there are rumors that Thane has established a base somewhere beyond the eastern reaches."

"The calm between storms," Seren said, taking the tube. "We'll be ready."

Above them, Stormwing and Seren's dragon broke from their patrol pattern, diving in perfect synchronization toward the lake surface before pulling up at the last moment, wingtips skimming the water. The sight—dragons flying free, uncorrupted, unfettered—filled Pryce with joy.

Together they watched the dragons soar against the starlit sky, the world poised between what was and what would be.

The End

DON'T CLOSE THE BOOK JUST YET...

Enjoyed the story?

If you liked Dragontide's Revenge, the best way to support the author is by leaving a short review.

Review it on your favorite store — even just a few words can help others discover the book.

Thank you for reading!

* * *

Want to read more?

Sign up for Connie Myres' newsletter and get updates, free stories, and exclusive sneak peeks:

https://www.conniemyres.com

Follow Connie on:

X/Twitter – YouTube

ALSO BY CONNIE MYRES

STANDALONE BOOKS

Twisted Intentions, Beneath the White Veil, Ring, Haunting of Ender House, Rest Stop Terror, Solus, Who Killed Sweet Violet?, Lucifer's Island, Raven's Ridge

DRAGONTIDE

Dragontide's Daughter, Dragontide's Son, Dragontide's Revenge

PACIE ROSE MYSTERIES

Pacie Rose Mysteries (Books 1–3) Slenderman, Hornet, Wolf Jezebel, My Name is Mr. Dibble

RANCOR

Rancor: A Paranormal Psychological Thriller (Books 1 & 2), Sinister Attachments, Unrestrained

SEVEN SEALS REDUX

Seven Seals Redux: The Complete Apocalyptic Novel Series (Books 1–7)

White Horse, Red Horse, Black Horse, Pale Horse, Tribulation, Signs, Trumpets

SUSPENSE STORIES

Suspense Stories #1: Raven's Ridge, Lucifer's Island, Sinister Attachments

WATCH FOR SPOOKY SHORTS

Spooky Shorts A-G: A Collection of Creepy Short Stories

Apple Pie, Black-Eyed Kids, Creature, Dungeon, Electric, Fairy, Genie, House, Ice, Joker, Kiss, Lucid, Minion, Neighbor (Upcoming: Obelisk, Pattern, Quest, Rumor, Squatch, Time, Underworld, Visitor, Wolf, X-axis, Yellow, ZoZo)

The complete list of books can be found at:

ConnieMyres.com

or

My universal book link:

https://books2read.com/conniemyres

ABOUT THE AUTHOR

CONNIE S. MYRES writes books and short stories in the horror, mystery, suspense, and science fiction genres. She is an author, developer, and registered nurse. Sometime in the future—whether by choice or by arm-twisting— she will join the digital nomad movement.

Born and raised in Michigan, she has been creating stories since childhood. Children she had babysat as a teenager loved to hear her mystery stories, especially since she carefully included all the children listening into the storyline, causing suspense for everyone.

Connie's website is ConnieMyres.com

FEATHER AND FERMION PUBLISHING Feather and Fermion Publishing is a Michigan-based publisher that was founded in 2014. Our mission is to provide readers with thrilling and entertaining stories across a variety of genres, including horror, mystery, suspense, thriller, science fiction, and fantasy. We publish original fiction under our two imprints: Oort Cloud Books and White-Knuckle Books

Author Connie Myres owns Feather and Fermion Publishing.